Alice Cary

Snow-Berries

A book for young folks

Alice Cary

Snow-Berries
A book for young folks

ISBN/EAN: 9783337254537

Printed in Europe, USA, Canada, Australia, Japan

Cover: Foto ©Andreas Hilbeck / pixelio.de

More available books at **www.hansebooks.com**

THE SPOTTED DEER.

SNOW–BERRIES.

A BOOK FOR YOUNG FOLKS.

By ALICE CARY.

WITH ILLUSTRATIONS.

BOSTON:
TICKNOR AND FIELDS.
1867.

UNIVERSITY PRESS: WELCH, BIGELOW, & CO.,
CAMBRIDGE.

PRELUDE.

MY little men and women
    Who sit with your eyes downcast,
Turning the leaves of the Snow-Berries
    Over and over so fast,

I know as I hear them flutter
    Like the leaves on a summer bough,
You are looking out for the story about
    The fairies, — are n't you, now?

And so it is wise to tell you
    That you need not turn so fast,
For there is n't a single fairy-tale
    In the book from first to last.

My Muse is plain and homespun, —
    Quite given to work-day ways, —
And she never spent an hour in the tent
    Of a fairy, in all her days.

She is strongest on her native soil;
    And you will see she sings
Little in praise of elfs and fays,
    And less of queens and kings.

The finest ladies, so she says,
    And the gentlemen most grand,
Are made by Nature gentlefolk,
    And are royal at first hand.

She says of the women who sew and spin,
    And keep the house with care,
That they are the queens and princesses
    Whose trains we ought to bear.

And says of the men who hammer and forge,
    And clear and plough the land,
That they are the worthy gentlemen
    Who make our country grand.

A ribbon, she says, in the buttonhole,
    May go for what it goes,
But he is the greatest man who is great
    Without such tinsel shows.

Our country's flag can never drag,
    She says, nor its stars go down;
For how should it fall when one and all
    Are rightful heirs to the crown !

But, little women, and little men,
    I will tell you now, if you please,
What I set out to tell you about, —
    Some real snow-berries.

All in the wild November,
  And a long, long time ago,
When the birds were gone and the daisies done,
  And clouds hung chilly and low,

Seven little and laughing children —
  I, as you guess, being one —
Stood at the pane to charm the rain,
  And to catch a glimpse of the sun.

At noon it was dreary as twilight,
  But just as the clock struck two
There broke its way through the mass of gray
  A hand's-breadth of the blue.

How close we pressed to see some cloud
  Put on a golden edge, —
Head over head, and cheeks as red
  As the roses in a hedge.

And the gray is grained with silver,
  And the blue has widened its streak ;
And I was the one to see the sun,
  And I was the one to speak !

" Now, out and away to the meadows !
  The rain has been charmed, you see, —
For here at our feet are our shadows, —
  Three, and one, and three.

" Be sure, the beautiful violet
   In the grass no longer glows,
But we may get a-burning yet,
   Some little lamp of a rose ! "

So out we ran to the meadows,
   Though the time of flowers was done,
And after us ran our shadows, —
   Three and three, and one.

All up and down the rivulets
   That shaved so close to the sand,
And all across the lowland moss,
   And across the stubble land ;

And deep, and deeper into the wood,
   And under the hedge-row wall ;
To the Callamus Pond, and on beyond,
   And never a flower at all !

Footsore, weary, and heart-sick,
   We had tramped for three long hours,
When a voice so proud cried out aloud,
   " The flowers ! I 've found the flowers ! "

Fast we flew to the top of the hill,
   And fast and faster down,
And full in sight limbs shone so white
   From the thicket dull and brown.

The turf slides back, and farther back,
   We are there, we are under the trees!
And our eager hands are breaking the wands
   Of the milk-white snow-berries!

We had had a tramp, through cold and damp,
   Of three right weary hours,
But we did not grieve, if you believe,
   That our berries were not flowers!

But each with a sheaf on his shoulder,
   As white as the whitest foam,
We struck across the lowland moss,
   And into the lights of home.

So, my little men and women,
   Who sit with your eyes downcast,
Turning the leaves of the Snow-Berries,
   So eagerly and so fast,

When that you fail to find the tale
   Of airy fancy bred,
You may even get some pleasure yet
   From the stories in their stead.

CONTENTS.

—◆—

PART I.

PART II.

PART III.

PART I.

THE SPOTTED DEER.

THE sun was growing large toward the setting, and the light, more red than golden, shining more and more faintly along a great mass of woods that reached backward and upward along the slope, till their tops seemed to touch the sky, almost, and the red and scarlet and yellow of the foliage — for it was autumn — to be giving their colors to the clouds, when an adventurer made fast his boat on the shore of the Ohio immediately opposite Little Sandy Creek; and, having given some directions to his men, proceeded, accompanied only by his dog, to climb the ascent along which the village of Lewisburgh was sprinkled.

The villagers, as the stranger soon found, were but recent settlers on the land, — a tract of twenty thousand acres, extending along the river, and granted them by Congress in consideration of the frauds and impositions practised upon them in their earlier settlement of the neighboring town of Galliopolis.

They were mostly French, or the descendants of French emigrants, — a gay, primitive sort of people,

half thrifty, half negligent in their habits, and
in some sort refined in their rudeness, and cultivated in their ignorance.

They were generally farmers in a small way, each
having a few acres of ground attached to his cottage,
upon which he raised vegetables, grapes, and corn.

Almost every house had its flower-garden, its
bird-cages at the window, and its pet animals
about the door, and here and there in the outskirts of the village stood a tent or a wigwam
where Indians, to whom this people were very
friendly, carried on their trades, — making baskets
of birch bark, bags of bead-work, and other articles
of a trifling and ornamental character. The cot-
tages were generally painted or whitewashed, and
together with the tents and wigwams gave the
town a romantic and picturesque appearance.

The sunset light, falling upon and brightening
the mists of the river, gave a charming effect to
the beauty which the landscape would have possessed at any time; and the numberless children
engaged in careless sports, together with a great
variety of pets, sporting with and among them,
completed the enchantment of the scene.

We have said the grounds about the houses
were devoted chiefly to corn and vegetables; but
the peach-orchards with which the surrounding
hills were planted afforded the chief source of in-

come, yielding as they do without much cultivation. They procured them coffee, delf-ware, cutlery, and such simple articles of finery as the women desired, leaving abundant time for those pleasurable and healthful activities of which they were so fond.

It was September, with one of those mild, cloudy atmospheres that have the balminess of spring, and with the shadows came the young people out into the gardens,— the youths wearing blue jackets and trousers, which their mothers had spun and woven for them, and the maidens, party-colored dresses made in the gayest fashions which memory or invention could suggest.

Some of the more sober matrons brought out their wheels, or needle-work, and, under the trees, continued sewing and spinning till the last light faded from the hill-tops, and the bright stripes that variegated the woods were lost in one general and sombre hue.

The older men gathered near these industrious housewives, and, as they chatted of days gone by, polished their guns or mended their fishing-tackle; while the smaller children instructed the pet animals, of which we have spoken, in various ingenious tricks, until, wearied out, they sunk on the grass among them, and fearlessly fell asleep; so primitive and simple were the habits of these people.

The strange gentleman, as he leisurely strolled from one part of the village to another, found himself the object of much respectful admiration and attention : the old women smiled, for he was handsome, and when do women cease to give such recognition to handsome faces? the old men lifted their caps with an exceeding elegance of manner, and smiled, too, a little less graciously perhaps, while the children ran up to him and made overtures toward acquaintance by presents of flowers and grapes. On the shoulder of one little creature a tame blue-jay would be fluttering, and give its noisy welcome, and on the head of another the paroquet, making such signs of gladness as it had been taught to make, and the summer duck and the peacock, meantime, would walk before him, spreading out their brilliant plumage as if in contribution to his pleasure.

This sociability and friendship on the part of the children and their pets begot in the heart of the stranger a sympathetic and kindly interest almost at once, and his address so won upon these unsophisticated people that they extended to him an invitation to sup with them under the trees, and afterward join in the dance of the evening.

From the novelty of the suggestion, our adventurer entered into it with great heartiness, and a vivacity scarcely exceeded by his demonstrative entertainers. Almost every house contributed its quota of milk, wine, and peaches to the little festival, while he himself furnished his share in white biscuits, which he caused to be brought from the boat, — a donation than which nothing could have proven more acceptable, the settlers having subsisted for several months continuously on bread composed chiefly of maize.

Never was supper more cheerful, never was gayety more harmless; and as for the stranger, it was rather as if some dear friend had come back to his home, than as though an adventurer were by chance amongst them for an hour.

Three youths were in readiness with flutes and violins, to strike up after the viands had received due honor, the lads and lasses, not without effort, having restrained their impatience for more congenial merriment till the rural repast was concluded.

By and by the moon came up in full-orbed glory. Hundreds of candles fixed in the trees contributed to the illumination; and such a picture of rustic enjoyment as was presented we can only hope to outline imperfectly. The women put away their wheels, the men their guns and fishing-tackle; young mothers sung their babes to sleep, and, laying them on the grass, covered them with their shawls, and leaving the faithful dogs to tend them, ran to join the dance with hearts as light as their

footsteps. All seemed young alike. Old French-
men, lively as their grandchildren, were capering
about in crimson caps; while their wives, in dresses
of the fashion of the time of Louis XIV., gossiped
with one another with still more animated volubil-
ity; and the young people of both sexes, habited in
holiday costumes, lit up the shady places with their
bright blushes as they "tript it to and fro on the
light fantastic toe." Numbers of the domestic animals I have mentioned followed their masters con-
fidently among the graceful and merry circles, con-
tributing to the picturesque and inartificial beauty
of the scene.

Among these animals were raccoons and opos-
sums, both as tame as young pigs; also a curious
little animal called the ground-hog, which could
never be so far tamed by any amount of kindness
as not to snap at the hand that offered it food; but
the most remarkable and perhaps interesting of
all the animals was a huge cub-bear, that was as
full of playful tricks as a monkey, taking from
time to time some one of the children between its
paws, and rolling and tumbling on the ground with
it as though it were going to tear it to pieces, and
may be devour it into the bargain.

Some of the Indian women and children drew
near and gazed on the scene with a strange mix-
ture of the grave and the mirthful in their faces;

and it was remarkable to observe with what fondness the wild creatures — birds and beasts — gathered about them. Here a youth might be seen with a wolf or ground-hog, and perhaps one or two other animals, between his legs, and there a young squaw, with all her black hair hidden by the splendors of the wings that were fluttering on her shoulders.

The Indian men kept mostly at a distance, but one rawboned hunter was persuaded at last to perform the war-funeral and the marriage-dance, both of which he gave in grand style; and so the festivities, or the more mirthful of them, came to an end. The old people, who had been sitting on the benches ranged along the walks, arose and went home, chattering and gesticulating as they went. The mothers took up their babies, and the dulcet symphonies fell to a lower and lower key, till by and by they faded down to silence, and quiet took up her melancholy reign.

The heart of the stranger was sad as he took his separate way to the boat that, curtained with mists, lay hugging the shore; for there is a power sometimes in the intercourse of a few hours that holds us like the friendship of years, and makes us feel poor and lonesome as we let go some hand whose single pressure has given us the assurance of a kindness that shall assert itself in eternity, if not in time.

1 *

He was half way down the slope, and could already see the yellow-capped heads of the river-waves, and hear the whistling and talking of the distant raftsmen as they paddled their slow way to the music of the whippoorwills, when suddenly a sound unlike what his ear was tuned to struck upon his attention and jangled to discord all his sweet imaginings.

It was not a sobbing nor crying, but a helpless, hopeless moaning that was more sorrowful to hear than either, for it indicated a heart, not so much crushed by sudden misfortune as wearied out by long suffering.

Standing still to listen, our adventurer perceived a rude habitation by the roadside, from the windows of which streamed no light, and about which grew no flowers. Indeed there was not so much as a tree or a patch of green grass between the doorsill and the highway.

A little way from this dreary habitation, seated on a mossy log, and mournfully caressing two beautiful deer that stood on either side of her, was a young girl, apparently in deep distress. One of these deer was as white as milk, with the exception of a few red freckles on the breast and one of the flanks; the other, was as spotted as a leopard. Both seemed exceedingly fond of her; and while the one was rubbing its graceful head against her bare shoulder, — jangling a bell which was attached to a shining collar it wore on its neck, — the other licked the hands which lay idly folded in the girl's lap.

Her feet had just touched that marvellously beautiful, but also sadly uncertain ground where childhood and womanhood meet, and perhaps the time and the situation lent their charm ; at any rate, she had that about her which drew and fixed the eyes of the stranger. He could not, perhaps, have himself expressed the peculiar nature of the interest awakened in him, as the sorrowful face looked out from its cloudy tresses with an expression of gentle appeal. He at once approached, and, under pretence of the greatest admiration for the spotted deer, made a proposal for their purchase.

Was there anything under the sun that would induce the fairy-like keeper of these singularly beautiful creatures to part with them for good and all ? How came she by them ? O, he was enchanted, especially with the more spotted of the two.

"Tell me, will you part with them for any price ?" And bending low, the stranger waited in silence for her answer.

"O no, sir," replied the young girl, speaking English with an accent that betrayed her French origin. "I would not part with them for a whole

lapful of gold ; they are my only friends ! " and
she caught back her heavy hair and bent her great
dark eyes upon the stranger as she spoke, with an
earnestness that drew him almost to her feet.

" Your only friends ! how can that be, my pretty
one ?   Surely you are deserving a kinder fate," he
said.

She did not let fall the gathered-up tresses to conceal the blushes tangling redly along her cheeks.
She was too ingenuous, and too unaffectedly friend-
less to receive from the stranger's words any
meaning, save that of genuine kindness. On the
contrary, she told him all her little story with a
confiding artlessness and simplicity that must have
touched the best feelings of his manhood, and made
him friendly if he had not previously been so.

When she was no higher than her spotted deer,
she said, her good mother died and was carried
away and left on the hill that stood up so dark and
so high between the yellow woods and the river, —
their few cows and simple furniture were sold to
defray the expenses of a long illness, and procure
something a little better than charitable support for
herself.

So slender a fortune was soon exhausted, of
course, and our story-teller, whose name was Eveline, was elbowed and jostled about, now here, now
there, — now in the way, and now out of the way,

— now in the village, and now perhaps in the wigwam of some Indian hunter, — drudging with the squaws part of the time, and shooting with the bow and arrow the other part. In the spring-time she spun flax, in the summer she carded wool, in the time of the grape harvest she gleaned, and, in short, did what she could find to do; for it is the misfortune of poverty, that it has not a choice even of its work.

At length she fell into the hands of the penurious old woman with whom she still lived, and for whom she spun all day, and far into the night sometimes.

" And where did you find these friends ? " asked the stranger, seating himself on the mossy log a little way from her, and doing his best to win her favor through the praises he bestowed upon her beautiful pets.

Then he told the two deer in a most playful way, what blessed fortune had befallen them when they fell into the hands of the little maid who was their mistress, and asked them if they loved her as so gentle and good a maiden deserved to be loved.

" O yes ! " answered Eveline for them, not in the least embarrassed by the implied compliment. " O yes, they love me with all their two little hearts ! "

Then, as she knitted up her long hair on her fingers, and ravelled it out again, she told him, with a generous eagerness to oblige, how she had been used to bring home the cows from the meadow away beyond the orchard, and farther off than he could see, and how tired her feet would grow in the lonesome path for the want of company, and how, happening one night to meet an old man who was peddling fawns, she gave her ear-rings in exchange for two of them, hoping by her spinning she should soon be able to replace the rings. " But I never have been," she concluded, with a sigh that betrayed her fondness for ornaments and the sacrifice she had made in behalf of her beautiful favorites.

" Suppose I should give you the prettiest pair of ear-rings in the world, — coral drops, with gold setting," — said the adventurer, unknitting her black hair from her hand and folding it within his own as he spoke, " what would you give me in exchange, — the two deer ? "

Eveline looked bewildered for a moment, and then tears began filling up her beautiful eyes at the thought of parting from her only companions. "No, no," she said at last, " I cannot give them up, for you must know, sir, they love me, and even the pretty ear-rings you promise me could not buy me that ; besides, the old woman, who is my mis-tress, would steal them from me as she did my red ribbon to-night, keeping me away from the dance. O sir, it was breaking my heart when you came."

And with a charming simplicity she went on asking questions about the evening gayeties, now bursting into tears at the remembrance of the sweet red ribbon with which her hard mistress had adorned her own ugly person, while herself was wrongfully compelled to mope at home; and now laughing and blushing at the stranger's eloquently expressed regrets that he should not have had the pleasure of dancing with her.

"Ah, but you will come some other evening!" she cried, with the eager hopefulness of one who had never known a pleasure like that; and then she said, if it would really please him to dance with her, she would weave a bright garland of flowers for her head, and wear her blue bodice and scalloped petticoat!

What an honor and delight she would have, to be sure; and would n't the young girls all envy her, and would n't the old woman who was her mistress grow black in the face as a cloud, with angry irritation! And as long as she lived the memory of that night would be like a blessed candle burning away behind her in the dark! What evening might she expect to see him, and would he not come very, very soon? How lovely she appeared as she waited with eager uplifted face for his reply, her cheeks like two red roses, and the beating of her heart making the ruffled cape that was tied across her bosom flutter again.

The stranger was evidently touched by the simple sincerity of the fresh young beauty, and bent his admiring eyes very near the roselit cheek as he explained to her the little probability there was of their ever meeting again, even for a single evening.

"I am but a rude traveller, my pretty one," he said, "in love with adventure, and liking the woods and the fields, the birds, the beasts, and the curious insects of the air, better than I like the homes of men and the tameness and commonness of civilized society."

If life could be all one moonlit evening, and all a dance, and if he could dance with her, why it would be very nice and pleasant, but that could not be; his boat was waiting even then on the near river, just beyond the green fringe of willows that she could see so plain, — waiting to bear him, he knew not where, but somewhere far enough away from her, he was afraid.

"No, no, my child," — and he sighed as he spoke, — "it is not likely we shall ever meet again in this world; but before long you will find a lover to dance with, and then you will forget you have ever seen the boatman who sits beside you now, I dare say."

"O, how can you say so?" answered Eveline. "If I am not to dance with you, I shall never

dance at all, but spin and spin till I spin me a
shroud." Then she hung her head and made no
effort to conceal the tears that came to her innocent eyes; and her lately happy heart ceasing to
flutter in her bosom, like a bird that is learning to
fly, lay there as still and as heavy as lead. "If I
had only the red ribbon to give you, so that sometimes when you happened to see it you might remember me!" she said, at last; "but the old
woman has stolen my ribbon, and that is the only
ornament I ever had, except the ear-rings, that I
parted with as I told you. Ah, it is too bad that
I have nothing to give you!"

Then the stranger told her not to fret because
the old woman had stolen her ribbon. "And for
that matter, you shall have another," he said, "if
you will only give me the deer. I can send it
with the ear-rings, you know." And then he told
her, seeing that she was not quite satisfied, lightly
touching her fair young head as he said it, that he
would take, of choice, one of the long shining
tresses that fell adown her shoulder. "And
would you indeed prize a lock of my hair?"
cries Eveline, in innocent surprise,; "cut it off
then!" And she leaned her head down to him,
singling one long rippling curl from the rest.

Such simple confidence was not to be trifled
with, and rising, the stranger said in an altered

B

tone that he must not deprive her of the shining tress, much as he would prize it, but that he still hoped she would be persuaded to give him one of her beautiful pets, — the one with only the spotted flank, or the one with the skin like a leopard, — just as she chose. "I know how much you love them, but for my sake!" he went on, — and then he said, no, not for his sake, but for the sake of those coral ear-rings all set in gold that he was going to send back to her! And while she hesitated, he said, perhaps just to say something, that he would have the spotted deer; and he fell to coaxing and petting it with all his might. The deer, being very tame, responded to his kind words by going close to him and eating grass from his hand, and by a variety of fond and playful actions which it had been taught.

"And would you really send me the ear-rings, and such lovely ones as you say?" inquired the girl, almost persuaded, as it seemed. Then her eyes fell, and in a changed voice she said: "But why, sir, do you choose the spotted, and not the white deer? I think, of the two, I would rather part with the white one."

And putting her arms around the neck of the spotted deer, she drew it close to her bosom, and began prattling to it in the tenderest manner. No, no, she could not part with that! The white one

was not so fond of her, and was surely not so pretty. Why, Spotty would follow her all day long.
She almost thought he understood every word
she spoke, and sometimes he would even come into
the house and lie by the side of her little low bed
all the night.

Then she made a confidant of her beautiful
Spotty, and told him that his little mistress loved
him better than anything else in all the world!
Sell him for ear-rings, indeed! No, not though
they were as big and as splendid as the new moon!
Then she did actually kiss the forehead of the deer,
and whispered something so close in his ear that
the stranger could not hear what she said, but
something that was doubtless very pretty, if the
dumb thing could only have understood it.

"And so you like your spotted deer the best?"
the stranger said, as soon as he could get the attention of the young girl.

"O yes, so much the best! Don't you see how
fond of me he is?"

"Very well, you may keep your Spotty. I think,
on the whole, I prefer the hind. Come, my beauty!" and he took the ear of the white deer in his
hand, as though he would lead it away.

Instantly the girl pushed off his hand and took
the head of the white hind in her lap. "No, no!
my poor Whity, your little mistress will not see

you abused that way, not she ! " Then to the
stranger : " She is used to caresses, I assure you,
and not to having her ears pulled."

" But I thought you said she was not pretty,
and you did not care for her," answered the
stranger ; " and I thought, too, she was my prop-
erty, and not yours ! Did you not bargain her
away for the ear-rings ? "

" No, I did not bargain Whity away at all ; it
was Spotty I bargained away, and then I took Spotty back, so that neither one is yours."

Then she began talking to Whity just as she
had done to Spotty before. " Suppose you are not
so very pretty," she said ; " is your little mistress
going to sell you away for that ! No indeed ! her
heart is not a lump of ice, and she could not be so
cruel, not for all the ear-rings under the sun.
Is it your fault that you are not beautiful ? No, it
is not your fault, but you *are* beautiful ! O, so
beautiful ! there never was a deer in all the world
so beautiful as my own little Whity ! "

She could part with Spotty best ; he was sturdy
and independent, and did not need her half so
much as poor timid Whity.

Then the stranger said she might choose between
her deer, but one of them he must have. And
then he drew a picture of Eveline in her blue bodice and scalloped petticoat, dancing on the green

with the very handsomest of all the young fellows in the village. "And what would you not give, then, for the coral ear-rings?" he concluded.

Here was a dazzling temptation. Would the stranger be very good to poor Spotty, just as good and kind as was his own mistress? To be sure he would; never deer in the world fared half so royally as Spotty should fare.

After some further talk, it was concluded between them that he should take Spotty and send back to her the ear-rings from the next landing-point. Then he took from his finger a small gold ring; would Eveline wear that in token of his promise, and perhaps, too, as a reminder of himself? It was a poor trifle, but he had nothing better to offer.

Ah yes, Eveline would take the ring, and wear it, — not in token of his promise, and not to remind her of a stranger. He would never seem a stranger to her, and she would require nothing to remind her of him; but for all that, she would take the ring.

So he took her hand, and when he had put the ring on it, said it was now time to say good by.

But Eveline kept the hand, like the sweet, simple child that she was, saying she would walk with him to the river-side, and watch the vanishing boat till it was quite out of sight. "And then I will go back alone," she said; "and then, and then, — why then I do not know what I shall do!"

So they walked together, the two deer following, through the mingling lights and shadows, and toward the misty borders of the river, which they reached at last, and could see through the swaying boughs of the willows the waiting boat.

A few moments they stood in silence on the shore, Eveline little guessing the charming picture she made, — the misty moonlight all round her, and the graceful head of her spotted deer beneath her hand, while the white one stood a little way off scarcely distinguishable from the surrounding mist.

" Be sure I will take the best care of your beautiful pet," said the stranger, as he was about leaping into the boat, " for your sake, my dear child, if not for his ; so you need not fear to trust him away from you."

Eveline was sobbing now, sobbing so she could hardly speak ; and all at once she threw her arms around the neck of her favorite, and, holding it fast, said she could not let it go ; he might have the white one, but the spotted one she must keep, she really did love him best after all !

" Then Whity it shall be ; come, Whity, my beauty, come ! " And the stranger began to coax and pet the white hind ; but she would not come, shying off and snuffing the air instead. Then calling two of his men, he told them to bring her aboard by main force.

"No!" cries the little mistress in an angry voice. "She shall go of her own free will, or she shall not go at all. I will never stand by and see her pulled and dragged from me as though she were the worst creature in the world, instead of the best."

"Then persuade her yourself," said the stranger; "you know how to coax her into anything, I dare say."

"Yes, but I will not persuade her to leave me! I have not so much love that I can afford to do that. If she is a mind to follow you, I must part with her, that is all; but I will never coax her to do so,—never, never!"

"Then I suppose I must go alone, after all," said the stranger, sadly. "And you, my pretty one, remember that you cannot have your white hind for an ornament when the day of dancing comes again."

"I shall never want to dance," answered Eveline, "not if I cannot dance with you!" And she lifted her face to him, all eloquent with its innocent sorrow.

Then he told her that her life could not be more lonely than his, going through the wide world,—in wilderness places, and in deserts, with only two or three rude men for companions.

By this time the white hind had come back to its mate and its mistress, and, drawing its head close to her, Eveline asked it in whispers if it

would like to go with the stranger and sail away
down the beautiful river, pointing as she did so to
the boat.   It was perhaps in answer to the motion
of her hand that the hind immediately stepped
nearer to the shore.   "Ah, then, she is yours,
sir," said Eveline, every word a separate tremble ;
" but I don't want the ear-rings.   I can't sell anything I love."   Then she gave him special charge
about the feeding and general keeping and care, —
indeed, a mother who was parting with her baby
could hardly have been more tender in her entreaties and directions.   "The poor thing is so
used to me," she said, " what will it do ? "

"There is one thing that you can do," answered
the boatman, " since you love your pet so very
much.   You can go along and be its keeper."

Eveline was smiling and blushing and trembling
all at once now, and the boatman went on : " I
see only one difficulty, I am afraid the pretty creature, being so fond of the mistress, will not care
at all about the master ! "

" But I will teach her to love you ! " cries the
little maiden, eagerly.

" And how, my lady of the woodland," answered
the boatman, " will you contrive to do this ? "

" Just by loving you myself," she said.   "There
is no teaching like example, you know."   And she
looked up in his face with a sweet sincerity, that
charmed the stranger more than he had ever been

charmed by any beautiful bird or bright flower, or by anything lovely that he had ever seen.

She would go, to be sure she would go, " But O, sir, how are you to get me over this wet sand-bar that lies between the bank and the boat?" There was witchery in the trust and the timidity, alike.

"Why, this way, my pretty mistress of the fawns," he answered; and putting his arm about her waist, sprung with her clear across the sand-bar and into the boat. Of course the deer followed, and directly all three were sailing away together toward the golden colors of the sunset, the master of the boat singing as they sailed,—

> "Night, with all thy stars look down,
> Darkness, weep thy holiest dew, —
> Never smiled the inconstant moon
> On a pair so true."

But there is no need to linger any longer; my young reader no doubt guesses the end of the story, and can make for himself a picture of the boat, as, dividing the silver waves below, and the yellow moonlight above, it bore away the artless and gentle keeper of the spotted and white deer, to the realization, let us hope, of brighter dreams than even the promised ear-rings suggested.*

* This little story is based upon an account which I found in a volume printed about sixty years ago, and entitled "Travels in America."

TWO BIRDS.

IN the blithe and budding weather
 Of an April-time of yore,
Two wild-birds sat together
 In the peach-tree at my door.

And each was gayly furnished,
 And in beauty all complete,
From the topknot brightly burnished
 To the rosy little feet.

Now under shadows winging,
 And now hopping forth to view,
To the other each was singing, —
 Thus the prouder of the two, —

Thus only, " Pretty ! Pretty ! "
 In a low, caressing strain,
While in answer, " Sweety ! Sweety ! "
 Softly sounded back again.

The buds to flowers were starting,
 And the young leaves came in sight,
While they stayed together courting
 In the peach-tree ; but one night

They vanished.   Swift with duties
   Ran the time into the past,
Till I found my truant beauties,
   As I knew I should, at last.

Making tender, twittering hushes,
   That were sweet as any words,
Flying in and out the bushes
   With a flock of little birds.

The snow stayed all unmelted,
   And the winds of winter beat
On the boughs that lately tilted
   Under rosy little feet,

When I heard a bird thus crying,
   From the cold and frozen ground,
To the mate above him flying,
   Half-distracted, round and round : —

" My wings are stiff and sleety,
   I am dying in my bed, —
I am dying, darling."   " Sweety."
   That was every thing she said.

TO THE BOYS.

DON'T you be afraid, boys,
　　To whistle loud and long,
Although your quiet sisters
　　Should call it rude or wrong.

Keep yourselves good-natured,
　　And if smiling fails,
Ask them if they ever saw
　　Muzzles on the quails!

Or the lovely red-rose
　　Try to hide her flag,
Or the June to smother all
　　Her robins in a bag!

If they say the teaching
　　Of nature is n't true,
Get astride the fence, boys,
　　And answer with a Whew!

I 'll tell you what it is, boys,
　　No water-wheel will spin,
Unless you set a whistle
　　At the head of every pin.

And never kite flew skyward
In triumph like a wing
Without the glad vibration
Of a whistle in the string.

And when the days are vanished
For idleness and play,
'T will make your labors lighter
To whistle care away.

So don't you be afraid, boys,
In spite of bar and ban,
To whistle, — it will help you each
To make an honest man.

COUNTING THE CHICKENS.

COME, Joe! come, Johnny! the chickens are out,
As true as I am alive!
Let me count, — one, two, three, four, —
O, if I can find but one more
Of the beauties, that will be five!

Just look and see how they hop about!
And see what a pretty thing
The little gray one is, and oh!
There *is* another one! see it, Joe,
With its head through its mother's wing!

My dainty darlings, be still, be still!
　　Just a minute till I can see
Which is prettiest, — that with down
Softly yellow and striped with brown,
　　Or that with the golden bill.

That one is cunning, with back and breast
　　Black as a raven, and so small, —
No bigger than one of its mother's eggs,
And the tiniest little rosy legs, —
　　I hardly saw it at all.

I will double up my hand to a nest,
　　Afraid though I am of the mother hen,
And put them into it one by one,
The gray, the yellow, the black, and dun,
　　And see which is prettiest then!

ADVICE.

DO not look for wrong and evil, —
　　You will find them if you do;
As you measure for your neighbor
　　He will measure back to you.

Look for goodness, look for gladness,
　　You will meet them all the while;
If you bring a smiling visage
　　To the glass, you meet to smile.

TALK WITH A TREE.

STANDING straight up in the glory
   Of God's sunshine, O my tree,
I would know thy wondrous story, —
   Wilt thou speak and tell it me?
With head in the sun and feet in the ground,
My heart it keepeth sweet and sound,
And evermore I grow and grow,
And this is all I know.

Rough and wild and many-jointed,
   Thou art clothed with gracious hues,
And thy body is anointed
   Nightly with the pleasant dews.
The sun and the storm I gladly greet,
And my heart it keepeth sound and sweet,
And my head is high and my root is low,
And this is all I know.

All thy blossoms come in season, —
   In their time thy fruits come in, —
Canst thou give to me a reason?
   Thou dost neither toil nor spin.
Deep I strike my roots in the ground,
And my heart it keepeth sweet and sound,
And my buds they bloom, and my fruits they glow,
And this is all I know.

From thy roots in silence pushing
   Through the dark and gloomy ground, —
From thy boughs with blossoms blushing, —
   From thy heart so sweet and sound,
Thou seemest to tell me, tree of mine,
We are not all earthy nor all divine,
But sown in corruption to be raised
Incorruptible, — God be praised.

A NEW-YEAR'S LESSON.

THE house was little and low and old,
   But the logs on the hearth burned bright,
And two little girls with locks of gold
   Were playing in the light;
And their hearts were glad and their laughter gay,
For the morrow would bring the New-Year's day.

The house was little, the house was low;
   But cheerily shone the light
Out of the window and over the snow
   (For the ground with snow was white),
Cheerily shimmered and shone about,
As if there were fire within and without.

An ancient, gnarled, and knotty tree
   Hung all about the eaves;

So the little house just seemed to be
   A bird's-nest in the leaves;
And the little girls, in homespun dressed,
Just like the nestlings of the nest.

And still as the wind with sharp teeth snapped
   A leaflet sere and brown,
Right merrily their hands they clapped
   To see it sliding down,
Past the firelight's ruddy glow,
To the fire that seemed to be in the snow.

"O mother, mother!" they cried with a will,
   Their cheeks to the window pressed,
And peeping shyly over the sill,
   Like birdlings over the nest,
"See how it flutters and flies about;
It thinks there is fire in the snow, no doubt."

And then they laugh and shout with glee,
   And tell how wild it whirls,
And call it crazy as it can be,
   "You foolish little girls!"
The mother sadly and sweetly said,
Laying a hand on each golden head: —

"Suppose that leaf a crazy thing,
   My darlings; even suppose
It thought the firelight glimmering
   Out there upon the snows,

2 *   o

The same as the fire upon the hearth,
Why, that were not a cause for mirth!"

And then she says, as pearl on pearl
 Her pale cheek trickles down:
" It makes me think of the beggar-girl
 We saw in the streets of the town;
Her hand as little and brown as a leaf, —
Just such a picture of houseless grief.

" By some sharp breath of fortune whirled
 Away from her mother's knee,
She is left to flutter about the world,
 The same as the leaf of a tree;
No roof for her, my dears, you know,
Nor fire, except the fire in the snow.

" In her poor hand, so brown and cold,
 No New-Year's gift will shine."
Dropped low was each shining head of gold.
 " I wish I could give her mine!"
Cry both little girls, as they see the glow
Of their New-Year's fire outside in the snow.

THE BURNING PRAIRIE.

THE prairie stretched as smooth as a floor,
   Far as the eye could see,
And the settler sat at his cabin door
   With a little girl on his knee,
Striving her letters to repeat,
And pulling her apron over her feet.

His face was wrinkled, but not old,
   For he held an upright form,
And his shirt-sleeves back to the elbow rolled,
   They showed a brawny arm;
And near in the grass, with toes upturned,
Was a pair of old shoes, cracked and burned.

A dog with his head betwixt his paws
   Lay lazily dozing near,
Now and then snapping his tar-black jaws
   At the fly that buzzed at his ear;
And near was the cow-pen, made of rails,
And a bench that held two milking-pails.

In the open door an ox-yoke lay,
   The mother's odd redoubt,
To keep the little one at her play
   On the floor from falling out;
While she swept the hearth with a turkey-wing,
And filled her tea-kettle at the spring.

The little girl on her father's knee,
    With eyes so bright and blue,
From A B C to X Y Z
    Had said her lesson through,
When a wind came over the prairie-land,
And caught the primer out of her hand.

The watch-dog whined, the cattle lowed,
    And tossed their horns about;
The air grew gray as if it snowed;
    " There will be a storm, no doubt!"
So to himself the settler said;
" But, father, why is the sky so red?"

And the little girl slid off his knee,
    And all of a tremble stood;
" Good wife," he cried; " come out and see!
    The clouds are as red as blood!"
" God save us!" cried the settler's wife,
" The prairie's afire! We must run for life!"

She caught the baby up. " Come! come!
    Are ye mad? to your heels, my man!"
He followed, terror-stricken, dumb,
    And so they ran and ran;
Close upon them the snort and swing
Of buffaloes, madly galloping.

The wild wind like a sower sows
    The ground with sparkles red,

And the flapping wings of bats and crows
  Through the ashes overhead,
And the bellowing deer and the hissing snake, —
What a swirl of terrible sounds they make!

No gleam of the river water yet!
  And the flames leap on and on!
A crash, and a fiercer whirl and jet,
  And the settler's house is gone!
The air grows hot.   "This fluttering curl
Would blaze like flax," says the little girl.

And as the smoke against her drifts,
  And the lizard slips close by her,
She tells how the little cow uplifts
  Her speckled face from the fire;
For she cannot be hindered from looking back
At the fiery dragon on their track.

They hear the crackling grass and sedge,
  The flames as they whir and rave;
On, on! they are close to the water's edge!
  They are there, breast-deep in the wave!
And lifting their little ones high o'er the tide, —
"We are saved, thank God! we are saved!" they cried.

PART II.

THE GYPSY FORTUNE–TELLER.

WHERE the bend of a beautiful river kept bright and green a little spot of this goodly earth longer than it stayed bright and green elsewhere, there used to be made, year after year, at the season when the leaves turn yellow and the mosses brown, a gypsy camp.

When the frost first bit the grass, and the rivulets hid themselves away, expectation stood a-tiptoe among the young people, and so continued, till some farmer's boy, perchance, riding home from mill, along the river road, would see the smoke of their fires curling and rippling high above the tree-tops, and hurrying home, would set the household astir with the news, — " The gypsies have come ! "

Then there would be whispering and laughing among the girls, and a missing of the lads when the family circle drew about the evening fire ; for it was the habit of the youth of both sexes to steal out to the gypsy camp and have their fortunes told ; and many a cock that had been used to crow in the morning, and tell the sleepy inmates of the farm-house it was time to get up and set the breakfast

in order, and yoke the steers, had to boil in some
gypsy pot to pay for it.   Among the vagrants of the
camp was an ugly old woman, known to the people of the neighborhood by the name of " Mother
Crow."   She seldom strayed from among the tents,
and was usually to be found, till after the middle
of the night, peeping and muttering over a great
kettle of simmering herbs, of wonderful power, if
she were to be believed ; and indeed some persons
said, who had watched her stirring her mess with
a crooked and thorny stick, that they had seen
sparkles of unearthly light rising out of it and set-
tling along her forehead like a row of stars.   However this were, she was certainly more feared and
believed in than all her tribe put together.   It may
be that her wisdom was made up chiefly of cunning, but no matter, — it passed current ; it may
be too that the snow-white hair, straggling from
beneath her cap of rabbit-skins, and veiling the in-
tense glitter of her snaky eyes, had somewhat to
do with her fascination.   She was very tall, and
upright as an oak sapling, but her dimensions in
other respects no one could arrive at very defi-
nitely, as she was generally loosely wrapt in a
big blue blanket, with a border of scarlet stripes.

Many a night the home-going fisherman rowed
softly ashore by the gypsy camp, to learn of Mother
Crow whether his sweetheart were false or true, and

paid her with the choice treasure of his net; and
it generally happened that he was richer than before; such exceeding worth is there in a happy
heart, and Mother Crow was apt to see the bright
side of things.

She could instantly tell, so she used to say, when
she stepped on the graves of persons who had been
buried a hundred or more years, but she could not
tell whether the ground she trod on were to hold a
coffin on the morrow or not.   She could see future
events, she used to say, but not the time at which
they would take place, and so she got along very
well with her prophecies.

Some persons, too good or too great to seek a
gypsy fortune-teller themselves, would gladly listen
to the gossip about her; or if they happened near
the camp at night, would stop and peep over the
shoulder of some lad for the sake of seeing her as
she sat inside a ring of eager upturned faces, telling all the girls and boys whether their sweethearts
had black eyes or blue, and whether they would
marry and make a journey across the sea, and come
back with a great deal of gold, and live happy forever afterwards, or whether they would marry, get
gold, and be happy without the great journey.

And it is no wonder these people thus stole a
glimpse of the strange woman, for she made such
a picture as one does not see every day in the

week, nor every month in the year, nor every year in ten.

Among those who visited her the oftenest, and upon whom she levied the heaviest taxes, was an old man who lived in a ruinous house by the river-side, alone, and whose strange ways had shut him quite without the pale of society, — in truth, he was supposed to have lost his wits, and was treated accordingly, when, by chance, his neighbors came in contact with him. The columns that once held up the porches of his house fell down one after another, and lay where they fell; the once beautiful garden ran to weeds, and, instead of flower-stalks, thistles stood up very high and proud; spiders made looms in the windows, and wove there all the day long, making curtains so thick it could hardly be told at night whether or not the old man's candle were alight.

And the truth is, nobody cared whether or not his candle was alight. He wore a shirt of patched flannel, trousers of an old fashion, and shoes quite distinct from the modern style; and instead of riding in a fine carriage he walked on foot. Perhaps it was not altogether his fault that he was shy and unneighborly, for certain it is, nobody stopped to inquire whether it were or not; and Mother Crow herself, skinny and haggish as she was, created a lighter sensation of awe than he. His hair hung over his shoulders white as snow, and his beard fell down his bosom in a profusion of silver waves, that contrasted strangely with the black and wonderfully inquisitive eyes, and made the children hang their heads when he came near, and older people too sometimes, for there was in his face, it must be owned, a look that seemed to accuse men. Indeed, he avoided men and women too, as far as might be; but when he could not help seeing them he was civil in spite of the accusing look, which, if it had been examined closely, would perhaps have been found to be distrust rather than accusation, after all.

"I don't like him!" people used to say; and it may be that they did not stop to think why they did not like him, and it may be that they would not have seen much to like if they had stopped to think, for we cannot very well see what is lovable in anybody till we first love them. Love not only sees existing good qualities, but creates good qualities.

All sorts of strange stories were told of this man, and in connection with everything belonging to him; this, among the rest.

One of the chimneys of his house had fallen, or had been blown down by the wind, perhaps, and the story ran that it had been tumbled down by the witches who were in the habit of seeking the crazy man's chamber by this means. Then it was reported, too, that a well of once sweet waters in his door-yard had grown brackish, and had petrified an ox that had chanced to fall into it, and that his horns might be seen any day sticking out of the well's mouth !

It is strange that such things should ever have been believed; but let a story once get afloat, no matter how improbable, and it will hold its place a long time in spite of everything.

The strangest and most improbable of all the stories related to the wife of the " crazy man," — for there was a time when his beard was not white, when his flannel shirt was not patched, and when he had as pretty a wife as was to be seen in all the county-side. Most of his neighbors could remember very well when the fallen chimney stood up red and proud as could be ; when at night there were lights shining through all the windows, so dark and gloomy now; and when the cedar beams along the porches, against which hung the gray muddy nests of wasps, were bright and sweet, and the rows of pillars white as milk. They could tell about having sometimes seen a gentle-faced and golden-haired woman walking in the garden, and how all the roses bowed their heads down toward her as she went ; and about the little child that she used to lead by the hand ; and they could whisper too, and they often did whisper dark surmises as

to what became of the woman and the child, for
they disappeared one after the other, and were
never seen or heard of more.

There were even hints of murder, and some
people said that the beautiful woman and child
were lying petrified away down in the well under
the stone ox !

But these things were only spoken under breath,
for all that was certainly known was, that a fair-
faced woman and a lovely little child used to be
seen about the grounds, and that they were seen
no more ; but that anything mysterious was con-
nected with their disappearance nobody dare posi-
tively assert.　But it was asserted and believed
that often, at night, strange and unearthly sounds
were heard about the old house, and in the end it
came to be thought that the old house was haunted
with witches, if with nothing worse ; so that often
when these noises were supposed to prevail, the more
superstitious of the people would shake their heads,
and whisper, apart from the hearing of the children, " They are the echoes of the love-ditties the
crazy man used to sing to the beautiful woman ! "
And then the windows would be put down and the
Bibles opened and prayers offered, and sometimes,
after all these pious ceremonies, a horseshoe would
be hung over the door-case to protect the household
against witch-work, so strangely are the minds of

men and women constituted. And at such times
the frightened children would look wonderingly up
into the faces of the old folks, and ask to have the
candles trimmed anew, or that another stick might
be added to the fire.

The story ran too, that often of winter nights,
when the moon shone bright on the snow that had
been drifted into fantastic but smooth curves along
the meadows, and in the ragged edges of the
woods, there used to be heard a footstep going
along their edges, — tramp, tramp, — and in the
morning it would be seen that the snow was written all over with letters which the crazy man had
traced with his finger, and the letters spelled one
name, over and over, sometimes a thousand times,
and that name was Hesther; but whether it had
been borne by the missing woman, or whether it
was a fantasy of his bewildered brain, was left to
conjecture.

The only person in the world for whom this sad
old man appeared to cherish any kindly regard
was Mother Crow. Under the straggling boughs
of an apple-tree he at length built her a house, a
very goodly house for a gypsy, with a roof and door
of pine planks; albeit there were gaps between the
logs of which it was composed more than wide
enough for the moon to peep through and see what
was going forward. Many a basket of bright ap-

ples he bore to Mother Crow's house on his shoulder, and many a bag of corn he emptied on her broad clay hearth; and once, at least, during every period of encampment, he might be seen leading thither by the horns a fat heifer or steer, and then be sure there was great feasting among the gypsies.

It was noticeable that during the stay of these people the old man always became more like other men, that he would smile when he met his neighbors, and sometimes speak to them, not only cheerfully, but with great good sense.

It was strange his lucid intervals should always occur at the time of the gypsies' encampment, people used to say, but they never inquired into the mystery, for the world generally takes but little interest in its old crazy men that live in ruined houses.

Scarcely a midnight came and went that did not find the crazy man by the gypsy's fire, bowing his white head beneath the skinny hand of the old fortune-teller, and listening to her muttering, which contained always one and the same story; and of course the story was all about the crazy man's wife and child, for she pretended that she could look back into the past and see what had happened to them, and she commonly begun her story something after this fashion : —

3   D

"I see a beautiful river with a border of fine trees, and moonlight shining along the billows; I see herds of cattle grazing, and a great house with porches white as snow; and now there comes to the porch a fair young woman, with curls down her shoulders bright as the sunshine, and eyes blue as a morning sky in May. She wanders toward the river-bank, leading by the hand a child like herself, but even more beautiful,—her eyes being like the color of the morning-glory, and the fingers fair as the fingers of a lily.

"And now there leaps from his boat on the river wave a man, sleek and bright and stealthy as a leopard; he approaches her with smiles and gentle words, but his feet are shod with evil, and his heart is full of all manner of dark things. Now he talks to her and his voice is soft and low as the voice of the wind when it talks to the violet; and now he sings, and the song of the nightingale is not so sweet."

At this point of the story the old woman would stop and tell her eager, trembling listener that she could not see any more until he had again crossed her palm with silver, and so having got more money she would go on.

"All the scene that I lately saw is vanished, but I see the same woman walking in the fields alone. It is a wild windy night, and the clouds are flying across the face of the moon, and the autumn leaves are blowing about withered and dry, and still the woman walks on alone until she comes to a black-thorn-tree, under which, on a little heap of stones, sits a gypsy fortune-teller, — a wicked woman as I can see by her wolfish face, and her long, lithe, snake-like body ; and now she crosses the palm of this old hag with silver, and she tells her a tale that is like a fairy tale, of the splendid fortune that is waiting for her in a far-off country, — how she shall eat from plates of gold, sleep on a bed of swan's down, wear her hair braided up with diamonds, have gowns with hems embroidered with pearls, ride in a gilded coach, and have a hundred lovely maids of honor to be about her and to tend her day and night, and all just for going with the stranger who sings to her so sweetly, and who, she says, is a man of honor and authority in his own country. And the eyes of the fair woman are dazzled, and she seems almost persuaded to go away with the leopard-like man, and leave forever her comfortable home and her good husband."

And here again, Mother Crow would pause in her story, and profess that she could not see anything more until she had more silver, and then she would say that she saw a boat sailing down the river, and seated within it three persons, a man and a woman and a child, and that the three looked like the other three which she had seen before.

Then the shadows would come between her and the boat, and her vision would grow dim, so she would say, and not till the old man had paid her more money could she see anything further.

Sometimes she would sit for half an hour holding out her rabit-skin cap, and not till she heard something clink in it would she speak one word. Then at last she would profess to see the beautiful woman sick and dying, and to see the child, grown to be a beautiful young girl now, standing by her bedside; then she could see the eyes of the woman closed, and a long funeral procession; and after this, no matter by what prices the crazy man sought to buy her vision, Mother Crow could see no further; though she always professed to be growing in prophetic wisdom, and quite sure that at the time of the full moon, or at the falling of the November rain, or at some other designated season, she should be able to trace further the history of the young girl.

And this was the secret of her power over the crazy man, as he was called; and by this means it was that the entire gypsy camp fared so well year after year. But the more liberal the old man was, the more the fortune-teller demanded; and at last one night when the fumes of her bitter stew had

THE GYPSY FORTUNE-TELLER.

gotten into her brain a little more than common, it may be, she professed to see the fate of the beautiful young girl. She saw that she was living in the castle of a nobleman, and that she was become a lovely woman, with golden hair and blue eyes like her mother's, and that she saw little shining letters along her forehead which spelled the name of Hesther. But in what castle Hesther was, and how she was to be obtained by the old man, she would not tell until twelve pots of rum had been ranged along her clay hearth, with a beehive full of new honey at their head. This request was no sooner complied with, however, than Mother Crow declared that her vision was become dim, and that the anxious inquirer must wait another day. Of course she had her way ; but, alas ! things turned out as she little expected.

Having feasted to excess on the honey and rum, she lay down in her cabin to sleep, and feeling presently that the lease of her mercies was run out, and that the pains of death were hold of her, she called the old man back, and taking from her bosom the picture of his wife, she gave it into his hand, and also a piece of yellow parchment written over with clumsy and curious characters ; but the eyes of love can decipher hard things, and the old man read all the parchment contained, as if it had been written by a scribe.

Mother Crow watched him as he read, and at the
close of the reading lifted up her hands and hid the
light from her eyes, even before death hid it, and
turned her face to the wall ; so fearful, sooner or
later, are the effects of wrong-doing.

It was all a lie that Mother Crow had been telling the old man, after all. There had never been
a man who was sweet-voiced and sleek and shining
as a leopard, there had never been a little boat
that rocked on the river of nights, and there had
never been any running away, first or last. She
herself had stolen the child in the hope of getting
money from the father by telling him where it was,
and how he could get it again ; but when it came
to pass, as it did, that the mother pined for her
child till she became crazy, and wandered away
and was lost to her house and her husband, and to
all who knew her, she was afraid to say aught
about the child lest she herself should be accused
of murder. She was afraid even to keep it any
longer, and pinning to its dress a paper that said
it had been stolen and was to be given up if the
father should ever come for it, or any one, bearing
a certain parchment which the said paper mentioned, she one dark night, having taken it a
long way off, shut it up in a rich man's garden,
where the gardener would be likely to hear its cries
and take it to the rich man's house, as indeed he

did, and here the girl had lived and was now grown to be a beautiful woman. She had meant always to tell the truth some time or other, but had put it off month after month and year after year, knowing that her palm would no more be crossed with silver by the old man if he once came to know where his child really was. And the story was never told until Death came and put her soul in torture that pressed the secret out of her lips.

And the red leaves drifted in a red heap over the grave of Mother Crow, and the rain beat out the fires, and the pot of bitter herbs simmered no more, and the winter snow fell and lay in smooth curves about the stone house, for there was no name written on it now, and no crazy man anywhere to be seen. All the windows were dark as they could be, the fallen pillars lay one across another along the porches, and the chimney, in a stack of ruins, frowned from the roof, and at night not a sparkle was seen to rise above it. Now it was that the corpse of the old suspicion floated up on the stream of gossip again, more black and malignant than ever.

The crazy man, in addition to his other crimes, it was asserted, had poisoned Mother Crow, and, lest they who saw him should murder him, had shut himself in his own house, and was slowly dying of starvation and cold. Some even declared

that they could hear him making the night hideous
by his hungry howls.

But no man and no woman sought out the truth,
or made one effort to alleviate the miserable condition of the old man.

All at once, and as by magic, the stone house
was transformed into its original grandeur ; the
columns stood in white rows along the porches, the
windows shone with curtains of crimson stuff,
mixed with satin, white as snow, — the stack of
ruins stood up in a high, proud chimney, and above
it, at night, there glittered a shower of sparkles red
as roses.

And every day, riding along the river road, in a
coach with shining panels, was seen the man that
his neighbors called crazy when he *walked* along
the road.   Magnificent horses, in the most dazzling
furniture, drew the carriage ; and by the man's
side sat a lovely young woman, who folded his
mantle tenderly about him with her sweet white
hands.

But the most marvellous thing I have to tell is
the change that came to the hearts of the people
when they saw the gold trappings of the horses,
and the diamonds on the white hands of the young
woman, — whose name was Hesther, and the ermine that lined the mantle of the old man.   The
proudest of them bowed down as he went by, and

saluted him as though he had been a king, and his wisdom and beauty were the continual themes of conversation and admiration. The white hair and beard that used to be thought so frightful were considered regal now, and the austerity that used only to excite derision fitted him right royally now.

In short, no man could be found to own he had ever believed the rich man to be crazy. On the contrary, every one was loud in the declaration that it had always been his belief that the owner of the stone house was some great person in disguise, and a very wise person too. And those who had affirmed most vehemently, when the stone house was ruinous and dark, that they could hear its crazy inmate howling with hunger, were the first to make feasts for him, and illuminations, now that his house was full of light, and his board beautiful and shining with plate.

Not a soul could be found to own he had ever believed the rich man's well had a stone ox in it, and only one or two simple and old-fashioned old women would admit that they had ever heard the story.

Every one who could afford it built a porch against his house; white beards became the fashion, and the rich man's advice was asked upon the most trivial occasions.

Thus ends the story of Mother Crow and the

3*

Crazy Man, and I hope the reader has been taught
by it two things, — first, that conscience will find
out your sins, though you hide them under heaps
of gold, mountain high; and secondly, that those
who make feasts for you and do you the humblest
reverence while your mantle is lined with ermine,
will be the first to cry out *Crazy!* and see you
starved if your chimney chances to tumble down.

THE COW-BOY.

DAY after day, when the tawny-bills
    Were twittering through the boughs,
"Sook! sook!" across the sunset hills
    He would call his mother's cows.

"Whee! whee!" and then the thrum and fall
    Of the clumsy meadow-bar,
And we knew he had found them one and all,
    "Mottle," and "Rose," and "Star."

A merry cry, and then a hush,
    And then a merrier ring, —
He had found a bird's-nest in a bush,
    And was happier than a king.

" Plash and plash !" and " Sook, sook ! "
  And tramp and trill again, —
He had brought his cows acróss the brook,
  And was singing up the lane.

Spingspang ! whish ! in the bucket cool
  And burnished silver-bright,
And then he had gotten his milking-stool,
  And was milking with all his might.

Clump ! clatter ! spinkle ! span !
  He had done with the milking-chore,
And was setting each shining and shallow pan
  On the watery " spring-house " floor.

Days went and came, and came and went,
  And over the sunset hills
No more his cheerful call was blent
  With the twittering tawny-bills.

But in the dingle and in the dell
  Deep silence held the rule ;
The little lad that we loved so well
  Was gone to the grammar-school.

Years came and went, and went and came ;
  He had made, or mastered fate,
For the little cow-boy's humble name
  Was the name that ruled the state.

LITTLE ELLIE.

DARLING Little Ellie,
　　Stout of heart and limb, —
What, I often wonder,
　　Will the future make of him?

Where will be the roses
　　That keep his cheeks so red,
When years with their temptations
　　And trials shall have fled?

Stirring with the morning,
　　As if he owned the farm;
On the floor at sunset,
　　Sleeping on his arm:

Torn and faded jacket,
　　Feet brown and bare,
Sunshine laughing in his eyes,
　　And tangled in his hair.

In his little bucket,
　　Helping milk the cows, —
Riding on the horses,
　　Tumbling down the mows;

Wading in the water,
　　Working mimic mills, —
Chasing through the meadows,
　　Rolling down the hills;

Making strings of elm-bark,
　　Stealing mother's yarn, —
All to see his kite fly
　　Higher than the barn;

Planning long aforetime,
　　With ambitious pride,
How, when snow has fallen,
　　He 'll have a sled and ride.

Gravely puzzling over
　　Each childish little plan, —
Working, and tugging,
　　And scheming like a man.

Now upon grandfather's knee,
　　Listening with delight
To the stories that are new
　　Every day and night.

Now, with joyous make-believe
　　In despite his frown,
Turning chairs to railcars,
　　And riding into town.

Ah, 't is wisely well for us
That we cannot see
What in years that are to come
He will grow to be.

THE BRICKMAKER'S BOY.

THE ground of the brick-yard is burning and bare;
   By the hedgerow are plenty of shady spots,
But Ralph, when he gets a white apron to wear,
   Plays in the mortar, and shapes it to pots.

That is his mother's house over the hill,
   With the pitcher of pinks in the window, so sweet,
And Ralph is her darling, and sets at his will,
   In the soft bricks, the prints of his bare little feet.

Poor soul! — she is homely and wrinkled and old,
   And work is her portion, but what does she care
For herself, since no neighbor has need to be told
   That her darling has beauty enough, and to spare!

Low down on the limbs of the prickly sweet-brier
   Are handfuls of roses, but still he will push
His cheek through the thorns, for the one red as fire
   That grows out of reach at the top of the bush.

Sometimes the old brickmaker, sunburnt and bent,
   Will tug him about on his shoulder awhile,
Whereat, growing restless instead of content,
   He scarcely repays the good man with a smile.

He makes of a stray piece of cedar a shelf,
   Sometimes, where he sets up his pots in the sun,
And then, growing vexed with his work or himself,
   He breaks them, and tramples them down, every one.

From the time when the locust puts on the white mass
   Of his odorous plumes, till in summer's decay,
His bright yellow jacket he throws on the grass
   And braves the bleak wind, he is busy each day.

I know it is all in his own wilful way,
   Yet sigh, as I see him a-working so hard,
His hands and his apron so heavy with clay
   He scarcely can toddle about in the yard.

My heart often says to me, wherefore employ
   Your thoughts in a fashion so pitiful? then,
Reflecting, I see in the brickmaker's boy
   A type of the work and the wisdom of men.

FAIRY FOLK.

THE story-books have told you
  Of the fairy-folk so nice,
That make them leather aprons
  Of the ears of little mice,
And wear the leaves of roses
  Like a cap upon their heads,
And sleep at night on thistle-down,
  Instead of feather-beds !

These stories, too, have told you,
  No doubt to your surprise,
That the fairies ride in coaches
  That are drawn by butterflies ;
And come into your chambers,
  When you are locked in dreams,
And right across your counterpanes
  Make bold to drive their teams ;
And that they heap your pillows
  With their gifts of rings and pearls ;
But do not heed such idle tales,
  My little boys and girls.

There are no fairy folk that ride
  About the world at night,
Who give you rings or other things
  To pay for doing right.

But if you do to others what
You'd have them do to you,
You'll be as blest as if the best
Of story-books were true.

LESS OR MORE.

SEVEN trees grew beside our door,—
  We used to wish they were six, or four!
Seven,— each standing so close to each,
The boughs from one to the other could reach,
And when the wild winds over them run
The tops of the seven trees looked like one.

There they stood in the rain and shine,
Like so many soldiers, all of a line,
Beating the tempest away when it came;
And still when the midsummer burned like a flame,
Dropping their shadows, now less, now more,
Over the door-stone and into the door.

Seven, and one of the seven, an oak,
Scarred and scathed by a lightning-stroke,
That, leaving it at the fork gaped wide,
Ran like a black vein down one side;
An elm, with a shaggy red vine at the top,
Hanging loose, and as though it were ready to drop.

E

Three sweet silver maples, a willow so fair
That like a lithe swimmer took hold of the air;
A walnut, too proud to yield ever a nut,
With all its black bark into rough diamonds cut.
And so there were seven — we wished they were four,
Or six — we would have them be less or be more!

Fair every tree of them — why should we say
If this one or that one were only away!
O, 't is no matter, — the story is meant
To show you that mortals are never content,
And if the trees had been six, or four,
We still would have wished they were less, or more.

FINE TALK.

THEY may talk about talk
        With a silvery ring,
But silence is sometimes
        An excellent thing.
Of course there 's no statute
        To limit the breath,
And he that so chooses
        May talk you to death!
But if you have nothing
        To tell or to teach,
There 's no use abusing
        The good gift of speech!

I ve heard tongues that clattered
  Like shallowest brooks,
But never the fine talk
  You read of in books!
I often hear things
  That were tolerably good,
But not your fine, fine talk, —
  I wish that I could!
For when words like music
  Have ravished the air,
It somehow has happened
  I never was there.

It is, as I fancy,
  The fault of my star,
For certainly somewhere
  Fine talkers there are;
And sometimes I 've thought,
  For a minute or two,
Here is one!   He was telling me
  All that he knew!
For when we next met,
  Without switching the train
Of a thought, he repeated
  The same things again.

And if I might venture
  One word to suggest
To the talkers, who brilliantly
  Prey on the rest,

I would tell them that no one,
   So far as I 've heard,
Likes always to listen
   And say not a word;
And that it were wisdom
   To ponder my rhyme,
And utter their oracles
   One at a time!

PART III.

THE WEAVER'S DAUGHTERS.

.

IN a poor little house that stood almost within the shadow of a great monastery there lived once two sisters, named Agnes and Elthea, — orphans, and heirs of nothing but an honest name and the trade of their parents, which was that of weaving. The elder, Agnes, had black hair, a pale face, hands that were never idle, and a tongue that was always still, except when it repeated prayers or when the prattle of Elthea provoked it to speech.

Mirth ill becomes you, good sister, Agnes often said, with severe voice and frowning brow. Do not the bones of our parents moulder in the dust? and have we not to earn our bread by our weaving? and if we take time to laugh, what will become of the work!

Then Elthea would answer something after this fashion : " I know, my sister, that you are wise and I am simple ; I know too that our parents are dead, and that we are poor girls who must weave from morning till night to earn our food and our clothing ; but I cannot see that it is wicked to keep the heart light just because the hands have to be busy, or for that other reason that our good father and mother have gone to a better world."

And having said this, or something like it, she would try to separate the smiles from her rosy mouth, and would weave very quietly for five minutes ; then, all unaware, she would break into mockery of the bird at the doorside, and after her little song, ask Agnes how it happened that so often at nightfall the cloth in her loom measured the longer !

" Giddy child," Agnes would answer, with never a smile, " do you not know that the Devil helps his own ? "

This was a dreadful thought, and, pondering it, Elthea would remain silent a whole half-hour sometimes ; but in the end laugh again, and reply, " If it be as you say, good sister, I will sing while I may, for the breath I use in singing would not serve me to cool the fires a thousand years hence."

" O my poor sister ! " Agnes would sigh, moistening the threads of her weaving with her tears ; and thus from day to day they sat at their looms, roses blooming in the cheeks of one, and wrinkles and pallor making the face of the other old before its time.

At twilight Elthea went with their woven cloth to the neighboring convent, where it was embroid-

ered by the sisters in patterns fine and beautiful
enough for queens to wear. If it were summer,
she plucked flowers on the way and made crowns
for her golden hair, which she sometimes wished
might be admired by eyes besides her own, as she
bent her head over the still places along the brook.

If Agnes could have seen how nicely she disposed
the flowers, and with what vanity she broadened
the golden bands of her hair, she would have
frowned, even at her prayers; but Elthea never
wore home the flowers. She gave them to the brook,
whose bright waters carried them lovingly away,
and smoothed back the broad bands of her hair before
crossing the threshold of the gloomy house, where,
till her return, the firelight seemed afraid to shine.

One night, as she was spreading the table with
bread and grapes and milk, singing a song so low
that it hardly came out of her heart,— a song that
was half thanksgiving and half prayer,— the great
bell of the monastery began to toll so solemnly that
for a moment she grew pale, and crossed herself in
silence; for she had been born and reared in the
faith that teaches men and women to believe there
is some special virtue in the sign of the cross, and
she had not learned that there is no virtue at all
in the signs, or outward shows of things. No
change came over the face of Agnes, and indeed
her face was always so gloomy that it would have

4

been difficult for it to look gloomier than common, but her voice had in it some bitter gratification as she said she was glad to see her sister Elthea silent and sad for once!

It was only for a moment, however, that Elthea looked sad. " I was afraid some evil had fallen upon the land, at first," she said, " but I perceive by the peculiar tolling of the bell that it is not evil, but good that has befallen. And it is probably some sister of the convent that has passed from death into life "; and so saying, she joined her little song where it had been broken off, and went on with her preparations for supper with a face as tenderly bright as the tenderest and brightest of all the May mornings.

" Hush! " said Agnes, lifting up her hand; " I hear the mountain wind coming angrily down; the roof-tree shakes its last leaves off to battle with it. Saints, protect us! it will be a fearful night! "

As she spoke the rain dashed against the roof as if a thunder-cloud emptied itself all at once. Then Agnes began to cry aloud, as a child that is lost in the dark; but Elthea said: " God, who holds the whirlwinds in his hand, will keep us, and we shall not die. Why do you fear, my sister? doth he not love us the same when to our weak vision the way of his providence seems dark? "

And still the bell tolled mournfully, the winds

drove dismally, and the rain beat heavily. It was enough to make any soul afraid that could not draw light into the darkness from the sunshine of a past life of pious cheerfulness and resignation.

"Have mercy on us, good saints!" cried Agnes again and again, wringing her hands in dismay.

"Our Father, we thank and bless thee for the fire that makes us warm, and for the roof that shelters us, and for our trust in thee that no storm can beat down," prayed Elthea.

Directly, in a lull of the storm, there was heard a knocking at the door, and Elthea, smiling, made haste to open it; for she said, "It is, perhaps, some poor wayfarer, whose life is mercifully given into our keeping." But Agnes reproved her with frowns, saying, "Stir not for your life; it is some murderer who seeks our blood, or at best a robber who takes advantage of the storm." And when she saw that Elthea would not be hindered from opening the door, she hid herself in the darkest corner of the house, under the cloth that was in her loom; and her trembling shook the floor beneath Elthea's feet, as her steady hand unlatched the door and set it open wide.

"Now, all good saints and angels bless thee for the sake of thy sweet charity," said the stranger who stood waiting. "I dreamed not these rude hills held so fair a blossom. Thy goodness—for I

am sure thou art good — shalt be my shield as well
as thy roof.   Bring me straight to thy royal mother,
that I may kiss her hand."

The youth and stranger had crossed the threshold
as he spoke, and now stood waiting meekly before
Elthea in the light of the burning fire.

"You honor me above my deserts, gentle friend,"
replied Elthea, her confusion showing all the more
for the blushes in which it tried to hide.   "We
are but poor girls, the children of weavers, and
our parents are dead."

"Children?" repeated the stranger, turning his
fair face toward the dark corners of the room; "I
see only thyself."

Then Agnes came forth from beneath the cloth
of the loom, and said, turning her dark face toward
the stranger, "My sister, a giddy and thoughtless
maiden as you may judge, has spoken truly.   We
are indeed poor, weaving all day long for our bread,
which at the best is scanty enough"; and she broke
the small loaf in two pieces as she said this, and
offering one piece to Elthea, began to eat the other,
for she hoped to drive the stranger away by showing him that they had nothing to spare.

But Elthea forgot her long fast, which she was
used to keep all day, and remembering the stranger,
who had been beaten by the rain, and must be
tired and famished, she offered him what bread
was left without tasting any.

The stranger accepted the bread, bowing so low that all his golden locks fell down about his face; and seeing what he did, Agnes not only frowned, but asked, in accents sharp and reproachful, how the poor could work without food. As she spoke, the piece of bread the stranger held seemed to grow into a whole loaf, and the part he gave back to Elthea was more than the whole she had given. And as they ate, the rain drove, and the wind blew, and the great bell of the monastery tolled and tolled. When Agnes spoke, she could hardly hear her own voice for the noise of the storm. Nevertheless, she said she believed the tempest had wellnigh ceased, and a favorable time was offered for wanderers, if any were abroad, to seek shelter in the neighboring convent. The stranger seemed not to hear or to understand her words, for he continued to eat his bread quietly as before. "Had we never so much charity," continued Agnes, "we could neither shelter nor lodge a wayfarer, even though we knew him to be a pious priest, let alone a vagabond of a minstrel, such as are likeliest to trespass on the poor."

Now the stranger wore the habit of a minstrel, and carried with him a harp, so that if he heard the words of Agnes he could not mistake their meaning. But he seemed not to hear her words. He seemed only to hear the tolling of the monastery bell; and as he listened, the tears filled his beautiful eyes, and ran silently down his cheeks. It seemed, indeed, as if the shadow of some great affliction were resting upon him.

"Your tears will not be dried by remaining here," said Agnes, "for we are poor girls who have no comfort for ourselves, let alone for strangers, and we sell the kerchiefs we weave for our bread."

But Elthea, when she heard this cruel speech, came softly between her sister and him, and in silence that was just as sweet as any spoken words, wiped his tears with her long golden hair. And directly the heart of the young man began to be lighter in his bosom, and he told the little maiden, as she strove to comfort him in her own gentle way, that the king who had ruled in his own country for years and years, so wisely and so well that all his people loved him and came to him in the time of their sorrow as though he had been their own father and not the king, was now dead, — dead and gone, — and all the land was in mourning, and all the bells of all the convents ringing dirges, and all the sisters singing funeral chants. Then he made a dark picture of the king's empty palace, and of the king's son, who in his grief had wandered to a strange country.

"And what is all that to a poor minstrel like thee, or to the poor daughters of a weaver like us?" cried Agnes, her words dropping like icicles from her mouth. "The kings may all die and may all be buried, but can we leave our work to weep, though they were twice dead and twice buried!"

And having spoken these chiding words, she climbed into her loom again, and beckoned her sister to follow; but Elthea, who had a mind of her own, sat at the feet of the stranger and wept, saying, "The king was a good king and a lover of his people, doing in the land the things that were lovely and the things that were right, and it is a wise thing and a just thing to pause a little and ponder upon the life and upon the death of such an one." And the burden seemed lifted more and more from the young man's heart, for the words spoken by the gentle and kindly maiden.

"O my sister! my foolish sister!" cried Agnes. "What is the king to you, whether he were good or bad, whether he be alive or dead?"

But Elthea, regardless of her sister's words, continued to sit at the stranger's feet and to weep, and to speak words that were sweet and pleasant to him. And the wind blew and the bell tolled, and the rain beat against the house, but the moments fled away as fast as the moments of a bright day in the middle of the summer.

And as the firelight shone upon the young man,

and Agnes perceived that he was fair in the face,
and that his locks were in their beauty like the
locks of the morning, she grew only the more
impatient and vexed and uncharitable toward
him.

"You may perceive how poor we are," she said,
"and that we have but one bed, which cannot be
divided"; and then going on more fretfully, she
said that strolling minstrels, she supposed, were
used to no better shelter than the oak-trees afforded ; and as for the harp, the thought of it was
displeasing to her, and she would gladly have it
out of the house. "What is the good of music?"
she said. "Would it help us to weave the better,
though we should listen to your harp till cock-
crow!"

But the young man still sat contentedly by the
fire, his eyes resting on the face of Elthea as though
it had been the face of some delightful flower, and
the glow of the coals made his beauty radiant, and
his curling locks like the brightness of a day in the
middle of summer. His milk-white hands were all
sparkling with rings, and the weaver's daughters
had never seen lace in their lives that was so fine
as the ruffle he wore upon his neck. And seeing
that he sat thus contented, and seeing the white-
ness of his hands, and the glittering splendor of
the rings that adorned them, Agnes, casting upon

him a look of scorn, arose and dashed herself
across the bed, and made a pretence of sleep; but
she did not sleep, you may be sure. Sleep is gentle, and comes not readily to the ungentle, the
cold, and the hard.

Then Elthea stirred the coals, and added fresh
sticks of wood to the fire, and made all the low
room, and the two clumsy looms, and the cloth
that was in them, and the yarn that hung on the
walls, to shine again, and bringing her shawl from
the beam of her loom and the pillow from her bed,
she spread them on the hearth for the stranger,
saying how sorry she was that such scanty hospi-
tality was all she could offer. And the young man
thanked her with his eyes so kindly, and thanked
her with his smile so brightly, that she went away,
and resting her head on the cloth of her loom,
slept never so sweetly in her life.

And all night the rain beat, and the winds drove,
and the bell of the convent tolled; but at last the
cold gray morning rose over the hill-tops, and the
face of Agnes, as she left her pillow, was black with
rage as the clouds, for there sat the stranger waiting to share the morning meal. In vain she scowled
upon him: he would not be driven away, but
leaning his cheek upon his harp, followed Elthea
with his eyes, as she went about the humble room;
and she, still freely as before, divided her bread

4 *   F

with him, and after that broke from her geranium
all its pretty flowers and twined them about his
harp; for he was going to the monastery to sing
dirges and to offer prayers for the rest of the dead
king's soul.

"The king was a good king, and he is dead,"
said the young man; "and my faith teaches me to
sing thus and to pray thus for the rest of his soul."

And when he went away, Elthea asked the Lord
to bless him; and it seemed as if the blessing came
back and rested upon her own head, for her heart
had never been so full of peace as it was that day.

"A pretty measure of cloth you will be likely to
weave," said Agnes, flinging her shuttle across the
warp so violently as to break her thread; "the sun
is an hour high, and be sure I shall not divide my
bread with you for your folly!"

Elthea was thinking of the minstrel, and hardly
heard what her ill-natured sister said. She was
thinking, not so much of his beautiful locks, and
not so much of his fair face, as she was thinking of
his beautiful spirit, for it was that which made him
seem so beautiful after all; and as she thought, her
fingers grew nimble, and her shuttle flew just as if
it had wings, and the hours of the day seemed almost like moments, and before she had dreamed
of it, it was night, and her task was done; and
while Agnes still sat scolding and fretting over her

unfinished work, she was away to the convent with
her full measure of cloth.

A long time she lingered, for the music of the
choir had never sounded half so sweet: the minstrel was singing with the rest of them.

Three days went by, and on the evening of each
Elthea listened to the music of the choir, and the
hour of her listening was like an hour taken out of
heaven.

It was an easy thing to weave now, for she was
weaving dreams while she wove her cloth, — dreams
that stretched away and away, she knew not where.

On the evening of the fourth day she missed the
harp of her minstrel, and the convent seemed to
her cold and gloomy, and all the world to be
changed. And yet it was changed from clouds to
sunshine, and from the moaning and beating of the
winds to the chirping and singing of the birds, —
the storm was broken up and gone, and the land
was smiling again. She could not stay in the convent, but hurried away as fast as her feet could
carry her; and coming to the brook she sat down
on the bank very sad, — it seemed to her as if her
heart was being borne away in its waves.

The waters that had leapt and prattled along the
stones for the three days past were murmuring and
moaning now; the flowers that had seemed to be
made of light now seemed to be made of shadows,

or of something still darker than shadows ; the grass had lost its tender greenness, and the air its balm. Her very face must be changed, she thought, as well as everything else ; and looking into the brook where the water lay still and mirror-like, she was startled to see there a face beside her own. It was that of the strange minstrel, who had followed her, and was peeping over her shoulder.

With a cry of joy she turned to him, all her heart blushing in her cheek ; and then feeling that she had betrayed an interest deeper than a weaver's daughter should feel for one whose hands were so much whiter than her own, she covered her face with her long loose hair, and stood silent and trembling before him.

Placing his harp on the grass by the brookside, the minstrel seated himself a little way from where Elthea was ; and when the moon came up and looked over the hill, she saw the minstrel kiss the hand of the weaver's daughter ; and then she hid her face in a cloud, for she thought it was not fair that she should look upon that which it was never meant she should see ; but when she had gotten over the hill and came nearer, she could not for the life of her help hearing what the minstrel was saying to the weaver's daughter, and the substance of what she heard was this. When he had laid his hand on her golden hair, he told her that if he had

THE WEAVER'S DAUGHTER.

any riches except his harp, he would ask her to go
with him to his own country, and to be his companion always.

But what cared Elthea for riches? she knew
how to weave, and it would be easy work weaving for him. And there, in the moonlight, they
plighted everlasting love with manifold kisses.

Many nights the bosom of the minstrel had been
the pillow of Elthea, and many days they had travelled together, her feet bruised and tired, but her
heart running over with delight, and her lips singing and prattling all the while, when toward sunset one day they sat down by the wayside to rest.
Then it was that the minstrel told his pretty wife
another story, the marrow of which was, that he
was no minstrel at all, except, indeed, for the season of mourning for the king, his father; for himself was the king's son; and the poor weaver girl,
who had shared with him her bread and her fireside, was henceforth to share with him his broad
and beautiful palace, and for the shelter she had
given him from one storm, he would shelter her
from all the storms of life.

And Elthea was loved and honored by all her
people as long as she lived, and many was the real
minstrel that blessed her name, and sang songs in
her praise; and many was the embroidered train
she wore that was made of the cloth she had woven

when a poor girl, and the cloudy days and the stormy days were always brightest with the blessing of memory. And to the end of her life Agnes wore coarse frocks, and wove cloth to make embroideries that she never saw, fretting and scolding at her sister's good-fortune all the while, and spoiling before its time the beauty of a face that might have rivalled her sister's if she had suffered her heart to shine through it the same.

THREE LITTLE WOMEN.

THERE were three little women,
  Each fair in the face,
And their laughter, like music,
  Filled all the green place,
As they sat knitting talk with the
  Threads of their lace.

Of the winds in the tree-tops,
  The flowers in the glen, —
The birds, the brown robin,
  The wood-dove, the wren, —
They talked, but their thoughts were
  Of three little men !

The sea lay before them,
  With ships going by;
Behind them the hills shone,
  So grand and so high;
And above them, blue beautiful
  Patches of sky.

But they felt not the sweetness
  That smiled from the lea,
And they knew not the way of
  The wind through the tree;
And they saw not the sea,
  When they looked at the sea!

The wood-dove tapped note of the storm,
  The shy wren
Twittered fearful, and low
  Hung the mist o'er the fen,
But all that they thought of
  Was three little men!

The wind rose, the clouds gathered,
  Mass upon mass,
The sun drew his long lines
  Of light from the grass, —
Alas! for the three little
  Women, alas!

Fast home ran the robin,
  Fast home flew the wren;

The blacksnake led all his
   Black sons to the fen,
That lay 'twixt the three
   Little women and men.

The sky was all over
   One horrible frown;
The rain from the hill-tops
   In torrents dashed down,
The three little short-sighted
   Women to drown.

They died: pray their watery
   Graves may atone
For their folly, in trusting
  · To see things alone
Through the eyes of the
   Three little men, — not their own.

PRETTY IS THAT PRETTY DOES.

THE spider wears a plain brown dress,
   And she is a steady spinner;
To see her, quiet as a mouse
Going about her silver house,
   You would never, never, never guess
The way she gets her dinner!

She looks as if no thought of ill
　　In all her life had stirred her,
But while she moves with careful tread,
And while she spins her silken thread,
　　She is planning, planning, planning still
The way to do some murder!

My child, who reads this simple lay
　　With eyes down-dropt and tender,
Remember the old proverb says
That pretty is, which pretty does,
　　And that worth does not go nor stay
For poverty nor splendor.

'T is not the house and not the dress
　　That makes the saint or sinner.
To see the spider sit and spin,
Shut with her walls of silver in,
　　You would never, never, never guess
The way she gets her dinner!

ELIJAH AND I.

THE house that you see underneath the great pine,
　　With walls that are painted and doors that are fine,
And meadows and wheat-fields about it, is mine.

On the stony side-hill of the woodland close by,
In a house that is not half so wide nor so high,
Elijah, my miller, lives, richer than I.

When I go to the town to pay tax on my land,
He sits by the chimney, his book in his hand,
And merry of heart as if money were sand.

Of the meadows about him he owns not a rood,
No stone of the brookside, no stick of the wood,
Yet ne'er lacked Elijah for clothing or food.

'T is good in his blue eyes the twinkle to see;
That the mill goes awry never troubles his glee;
'T is I that must pay for the mending, — not he.

He laughs while I frown, and he sings while I sigh,
The pleasant love-ditties of days that are by;
So Elijah, my miller, is richer than I.

A FISHERMAN.

A FISHERMAN leaned on a clapboard gate
He was often used to pass;
'T was sunset, and two little boys
Were playing on the grass.

The watchdog by the door-stone sat,
   And bayed the rising moon,
And the mother milked her cow and sung
   An old and pleasant tune.

The children left their play and ran,
   And, leaning on her knee,
She milked the milk into their mouths,
   Laughing with girlish glee.

And as she carried her frothy pail
   Slow to the rustic door,
One little one held at her skirt behind,
   And the other one before.

She stopped, and hugging both their heads
   Against her loving breast,
They looked like two bright little birds
   A-peeping from one nest.

The sunburnt fisher went his way,
   Sighing, alas, alas !
It was not for the little boys
   That played upon the grass.

And when he came where cold gray stones
   Were standing, many a pair,
He put his net from his shoulder down, —
   His little boy was there.

AMY TO HER FLOWERS.

MY lowly little beauties,
   Your time is coming on, —
The meadows will be full of you
   Before a month is gone.
I never knew your names, so near
   Your wild estate I grew,
But would that you could be alive
   To feel my love for you.

Full many a time the coverlets
   Of grass from off your beds
I 've turned, my beauties, just to touch,
   With reverent hands, your heads.
They called you simple country flowers,
   But what for that care I ?
I loved you all the more because
   You were not proud and high !

We had our ways of naming you, —
   We children of the wood, —
Red-slippers, lily-fingers,
   Queen's cap, and martyr's blood.
The rustic flower, by virtue of
   A coat as brown as sand,
And by the dew-drop shining
   Like a sickle in his hand.

The crumply cow, — the little shrew
  In strange and sad attire, —
Lover's tremble, old maid's thimble, —
  Moon men, — miser's fire;
And one we used to gather
  When the millet land was ploughed,
With little thin and ragged leaves,
  We called the beggar's shroud.

The belle, — the lady leopard, —
  The sweetheart, — tender-eyed, —
The spinner's gown, — the winter-frown,
  And many a one beside.
And these, our untaught fancies,
  So much from nature grew,
I do not care to call you
  By the names that others do.

But O my little beauties,
  Of field and brook and brake, —
The slender ones, — the tender ones, —
  I would, for my love's sake,
I could take and make immortal,
  With the power of better lays,
All your crooked little bodies
  That had never any praise.

AUTUMN THOUGHTS.

WHEN frosts begin the leaves to blight,
   And winds to beat and blow,
I think about a stormy night
   Of a winter long ago.

The clouds that lay, when the sun went down,
   In a heap of blood-red bars,
Turned, all at once, of a grayish brown,
   And ran across the stars.

And the moon went out, and the wind fell low, —
   And in silence everywhere
The fine and flinty flakes of snow
   Slipped slantwise down the air.

Slipped slantwise down, more fast and fast,
   And larger grew amain,
Till the long-armed brier-bush, at last,
   Was like a ghost at the pane.

A group of merry children we,
   As any house can show;
The very rafters rang with glee,
   That night, beneath the snow.

The candle up and down we slid,
  To make our shadows tall ;
And played at hide-and-seek, and hid
  Where we were not hid at all.

We heaped the logs against the cold,
  And made the chimney roar ;
And told the stories we had told
  A thousand times before.

We ran our stock of riddles through, —
  Nor large, be sure, nor wise ;
And guessed the answers that we knew,
  And feigned a glad surprise.

But, in despite our frolic joys,
  That rang so wild and high,
We wished, we foolish girls and boys,
  That time would faster fly.

And years have come and gone since then ;
  And the children there at play,
Are sober women, now, and men,
With heads that are growing gray.

But their hearts will never be so light,
  And their cheeks will never glow
As they did upon that stormy night,
  In the garret rude and low.

PART IV.

THE MAN WHO STOLE A COW.

THE MAN WHO STOLE A COW.

THERE once lived in a beautiful country, no matter just where, a young man whose name was David. From his boyhood he was given to idleness and to dreaming, so much so that he came to be called by those who knew him Davy Dreamer, and it was predicted of him that he would never come to any good. But he did come to some good; he married a good wife, and a pretty one too. She was the daughter of a man as poor as himself, but she had habits of industry, and great good sense, which was a good deal better than a dowry of gold or silver; and it was, no doubt, more owing to her management and hard work — for she was never idle — than to anything of his doing, that, at middle life, Davy Dreamer owned a neat cottage and five acres of garden ground. Moreover, it is quite certain that not a flower-bush nor a sweet-scented herb grew on the little farm, if so it might be called, which was not of her planting. A woman who found no time for dreaming was the wife of David. Nevertheless, she was never heard to rate her good man for his indulgence in his favorite pastime, and never seen to frown, and some persons believed it was her smiling which made her face so pretty.

I said at middle life they owned a pretty cottage and a garden, which with careful cultivation would have yielded not only a competence, but many of the luxuries of life ; but I am sorry to record that David fell a-dreaming often, at which times the spade was sure to fall out of his hands, and as the pretty-faced woman who was his wife had tasks in the house to do, thistles grew up, and briers and rank grass choked the small vegetables quite down sometimes.

As a natural consequence of this thriftlessness, their wants grew faster than the means of supplying them ; for the little house was full of children — I know not how many, but so many that David often desponded and said to his wife in a half-dreaming state, — that it was quite impossible for one little garden to maintain them all ; and so he would sit for hours musing and meditating on what could be done for the prevention of want, — of actual starvation in fact.

" There will be some way provided, never fret," the good wife would answer ; " there are more berries ripe than I can get to the market " ; or, " I have found two new hen's nests, both full of white, fresh eggs," she would say to him, though most

likely he heard her not, and often it is supposed
he saw not the things which she did for his comfort and for the good of his children; for when
the cottage wall was newly whitewashed it was the
same to him as before, apparently, and when a
pudding was boiled for Sunday, or a plum-cake
baked, David took them as matters of course, and
ate them without seeming to distinguish them from
coarse bread.

If this were so, it was a pity; but I am afraid it
was so, for we have all of us seen Davy Dreamers
who took the favors that were done them as matters of course. We expect pigs to eat the acorns
without looking up to see who thrashes them down;
but we have a right, I think, to expect a little
more politeness of men and women. However, the
sweet disposition of the wife of David could not be
soured by any neglect on his part, and, indeed, as
he grew impatient and fretful and fault-finding,
she grew still more and more patient and gentle
and loving, — more industrious and painstaking
she could not have been.

Sometimes, when she asked David to assist in
digging the ground or in picking the berries, he
would answer, "Don't disturb me now, my dear,
I am making a great plan"; and so it often happened that she picked and digged alone.

At last, one day when the good woman came

home from market with some money in the bottom
of a tow bag, which she had got in exchange for
her fruits and such other articles as she had to
sell, she ventured to ask David what he had been
dreaming about. She had never been known to
trouble him so much before, therefore it is reason-
able to suppose that his vision had been unusually
extended.

"Why," said he, "I have been thinking that
some of the rich folks about here might give us
a cow and never miss her, and I am told there is
a man living on the other side of the island" (it
appears that David lived on an island) "the hills of
whose farm are all covered with cattle. Now, if
I go to him and tell him how poor we are, and
how much one cow would be to us, do you not
think he would give us one?"

But the wise woman saw no probability of such
good fortune. It was barely possible, she said, but
the experiment was not worth trying; and even if
successful, the mortification of having been a beggar would imbitter the cow's milk. The wife of
David, it would seem, had her own little pride, and
in my opinion she was all the better for it.

After this Davy Dreamer dreamed almost of
nothing but cows, and when he talked it was all
about the rich man at the other end of the island,
who had meadows against meadows all dotted over

with beautiful cattle. "He would never miss a
cow; and I dare say if he only knew of our poverty,
he would gladly give us one!" he used to say; and
once or twice he hinted to his wife that she might
go to him a-begging. But she only smiled and let
him alone with his dreaming, for she thought it
quite harmless. She had no idea of begging, however, for her part, and for days and weeks and
months worked on, and each return from the market town saw more and more silver money in the
tow bag. She was never heard to complain, but
often to sing, and often to discourse merrily with
her children, who were growing to be blooming
men and women. A nice little plan of her own
had the wife of Davy the dreamer.

Meantime, his head was filled with all sorts of
vain imaginings. Night after night he would start
up out of sleep, crying out, "Just see what a pail-
ful!" and morning after morning when he awoke
he would peep into the garden to see if a cow were
not browsing the cabbages. For hours and hours
he would sit facing the highway, wasting the time
that he should have used for working; and never
a stranger passed along but that he looked wistfully after him, for each one he supposed to be the
rich man from the other side of the island come to
give him the cow.

But morning after morning came and no cow

was found to be browsing in the garden, and stranger after stranger passed along, but if the rich man from the other side of the island were among them he made no pause. And all the time he grew more and more fretful and dissatisfied. He fretted at his wife, and fretted at his children, and fretted at everything.

"What is it troubles you, Davy?" the good wife used to say; but he would always answer, "Nothing, nothing!" so short and cross that she was glad to leave him alone. And then, while he covered his face from the light and moped and moped, she would go forth into the sunshine and work and sing, and make the best of things, bad as they were. "Never mind what father does!" she used to say to the children when they complained. "If father does n't help us, it is our place to get along without his help, that is all. We must none of us wait for another, nor depend on another, but each do his own work in the world, and do it cheerfully; and then, let who will be at fault, we are not."

"Your father will get over his delusions by and by," she would say, and she really had some reason for this hope: for at last he ceased to tell his dreams. But, alas! if she had known it, it was not because he had ceased to dream. He did not tell them, because they were evil, that was all. If his wife would not hear of his begging, how much less would she hear of what he meant to do now?

It is probable that to his own mind he justified himself, for the mind must work just as the brook must run, else it grows dull and stagnant, and reflects nothing clearly; and it is an easy thing for those who do nothing but dream to let their dreams delude them at last. It is likely that he came to think he was not going to steal at all, but just to take what he had a right to. He was poor and wanted a cow, and the rich man on the other side of the island would not miss her! That, I say, is likely the way he talked to himself, till he came to think stealing was no stealing at all.

And while he was doing nothing but make his bad plans, his wife was working and saving, so that the tow bag had come to have a good deal of silver in it; and one bright morning in May, when Davy had been turning and twisting and groaning all night, she arose early, and having arrayed herself in her best gown and shawl, told him that she was going to the market town, but that she was not coming back by the direct road, and might not be home till midnight. "And you must not be frightened, Davy," she said, "if I should not be home till moonset. I am going to do something that will surprise you, I think." Davy expressed no curiosity about what she was

5*

going to do, but he seemed wonderfully pleased that she was not coming home till midnight, and said a good deal to make it appear that the drive after nightfall would be much pleasanter than before.

She was surprised and a little disappointed at this, for she had hoped that he would miss her, and would, at least, ask her why she should be away so long; but she could not but see that her absence would be agreeable to him.

"Perhaps he is sick, and perhaps he is dreaming again," she said to herself by way of excusing him, and so kissed him and departed, but with a heart much less light than it would have been if he had said one loving word.

The old clock in the corner had not counted many minutes after the wife was gone, till the husband, having hastily prepared himself, took his way to the other side of the island.

He walked vigorously on, for the morning air was sweet, and a new project is apt to impart new energy. Gayly sung the blackbirds, hopping along the newly ploughed ground and up and down the fences, and the bluebirds twittered and fluttered almost in his face; and it was not yet noon when he came to the other side of the island, and found that the rich man's possessions had not been overestimated. Lying in the faint shadows of the trees

there were cows; standing knee-deep in the water
of the brooks there were cows; and grazing along
the green, thick grass of the hills there were cows,
— all with great udders, and looking so gentle and
so pretty. He saw, too, the fine house in which the
rich man lived; it was not much like his cottage,
and its splendor seemed to mock his poverty, so
that he grew angry as well as discontented.

There was no person in the field nor in sight, so
that he might have driven one of the cows away
quite safely, as it appeared; but though he broke a
goad from a thorn-tree for that purpose, something
seemed to hold him back, and not until nightfall
could he persuade himself to single one from the
number and drive her away. But when at last
the sun was down and the shadows began to dark-
en, there came into the field the keeper of the
cows and called them home to be milked; and
Davy, who had been waiting all day for this favor-
ing hour, was half glad when he saw the coveted
opportunity passing away. But it seems that when
our hand is once lifted up to do evil, Satan stands
ready to take it, and to lead us; and what we call
chance favored the man's bad designs.

One of the cows, unmindful of the call of her
master, stayed feeding along the hollow and was
not missed among so many. Suddenly the clouds,
which had been floating about during the day,

darkened together ; so that but for the white face of the cow, the old man could not have seen her a dozen yards away. Summoning up all the resolution of the growth of years, he drove her with the thorn-goad away from her own home. Many times he paused and listened, thinking he heard footsteps pursuing him ; and many times he hid in the thickets, for he thought voices called him to stop, and if the harmless cow but turned her face toward him and lowed, he almost shrieked aloud ; so trembling and listening, and framing lies to tell to his good wife when he should reach home, he crept slowly forward.

Having fasted all day, he grew faint, and the unaccustomed exercise had made him tired, so that he resolved to rest for a time and drink some of the cow's milk, and at the rising of the moon, which he apprehended would scatter the clouds, go on refreshed.

Under the shelter of a low-spreading beech, upon which the dead leaves of the last year hung thick, he stopped ; and taking a small but stout cord from his pocket, secured the cow, tying her by the horn to the trunk of the tree. She seemed very gentle and quiet, but, though he knew not why, he could not make up his mind to taste her milk, hungry and tired as he was ; so leaning against the tree, he resolved to wait the rising of the moon, and to take a nap meantime.   But this resolve was much easier made than executed.   Sleep would not come to him for any scolding or fretting, as his wife had always been used to do.   It was not because his bed was the ground, and not because his grass pillow could not be moved like his feather one at home, that he could not sleep, — though he tried to make himself believe so; it was because he had done that which he should not have done that he could not sleep.

It seemed to him that every step he heard was the step of some one coming to arrest him; and his imagination made pictures of prison walls, of jailers, and of everything that was frightful to think of.   The very moon seemed to look reproachfully on him from the sky, and to say: "You are a thief, old man! and you had better go and jump into the river, if you can't be an honest man!"

The corn-blades, as they rustled, seemed to him to be talking to him, and to say: "Have you ever made a cornstalk grow or an apple-tree bloom and bear? have you planted a wheat-field or sown a meadow, or done anything else to help the world along, or to make it any the better for your having lived?"   In the leaves of the tree under which he was lying, the wind seemed to stop and to stay there, fretting and scolding; he had always thought the wind murmured and sung before, but it cer-

tainly scolded now. The voice that used to whisper in the leaves seemed now to be saying, " I am
ashamed of you! I am ashamed of you!" over
and over and over. Poor old man! he was
ashamed of himself, and that was why the wind
took such a sound.

Two crows alighted near by him, on the dead
branch of an old tree, and though it was not the
time for them to make a noise, being night, they
set up a cry; but instead of saying Caw! caw! as
is the way of crows, they seemed to Davy to be
saying Cow! cow! So that he concluded that
they too knew what he had done. And more than
this, he thought everybody would hear them, and
the whole world would know of it.

He wished he had never heard of the rich man;
he wished he had stayed at home and minded his
own business, and never seen a cow, nor heard of
a cow, nor thought of a cow! but above all, he
wished that he had not stolen a cow! Sometimes
he was almost persuaded to drive her back, turn
her into her own green pasture, go home to his
good wife and confess all the truth, and try to be a
better man; but it is hard to turn evidence against
ourselves, and the man who has lied once will generally tell forty other lies to conceal the one, rather
than own the simple truth. I suppose a man never
suffered more from the torment of conscience than

Davy the Dreamer suffered as he lay there on the ground by the side of his cow. And yet she looked so beautiful as she stood there chewing the cud in the moonlight, he could not help the thought, now and then, that she would be a great delight to him if he once had her in his own pasture, and if he could be sure that no living mortal would ever know how he came by her! But even this fancy did not quite satisfy him. "There is one person that will know," said he, "and that is myself! O, misery, misery! if I could only bribe my own thoughts to let me alone!" But this Davy could not do, for no man ever could do it; and feeling how impossible it was to have his own respect, to have anything but his own condemnation, he trembled and hid his face in the wild grass about him like a frightened beast.

At last the full moon got over the trees and the hills and the low clouds, and in the clear sky shone out in full splendor. And with the beautiful light some part of his awful fear vanished; and having listened, and hearing no step, and the crows being now still, he softly untied the cow and drove her homeward. He did not get on very far, however, before he found that he had lost his way. In the first place, he had never been from home, and did not know the roads; and in the next, his mind was so full of terror as to bewilder him, and in fact

make him almost like a crazy man. He could not
tell north from south, nor east from west, and when
he came to where the roads forked, he could not
for the life of him conclude which way to go. So
he drove his cow into the woods, tied her to a tree,
as before, and resolved to wait till morning.

By and by the cow lay down among the dry
leaves, and her deep quiet breathing, together with
the security of the place, soothed Davy, so that he
at length lay down beside her, and, nestled close to
her speckled hide, fell asleep, and in his sleep he
dreamed, and this was what he dreamed.

It seemed to him that he got safely home with
his cow, even to the garden gate. And that on
looking up he saw that his house was burned down;
and while he stood in consternation, one of his
neighbors met him and told him that his wife was
dead of a broken heart, and that his children were
some of them run away, and some of them in prison
for stealing cows!

He awoke with a stifled cry in his heart, and sitting up, saw that it was daylight, and that the gray
dew was lying all over his hair and clothes; his
limbs were stiff, and he was chilled through and
through.

A squirrel near by was chattering among the
tangled roots of an old tree, and it seemed to Davy
that he kept saying, " Good for you ! good for you !

THE MAN WHO STOLE A COW.

good for you!" So that it was all.the same with him, whether asleep or awake there was no peace.

When he tried to walk his legs dragged under him as if they were half asleep, and his mind was benumbed as well as his body; but still it was filled with strange, crazy notions that tormented him cruelly.

A little way from where he had passed the night there was a mossy stone sticking up out of the ground, three times as big as his head, and at one moment he was tempted to wrench this stone out of its place, and knock the cow on the head with it: if she were only dead, it seemed to him that that would make it as if he had not stolen her.

Chilled, hungry, bewildered, half crazy, he knew not what to do, for he was just as much lost as he had been in the dark. Sometimes he thought he would go and give himself up as a thief; still he did not, nor did he do anything else except stagger blindly about, and almost wish himself dead and buried under the dry leaves of the forest.

By and by the cow got hungry too, and pulled at the rope with which she was tied, and lowed again and again; so loud that Davy thought somebody would certainly hear her, and come and take her away, and himself too, with iron handcuffs on!

At length, he struck the cow in his rage because

H

she lowed so loud, and suddenly jerking at the rope with which she was tied, she broke it, and ran away. Now Davy no sooner saw her escaping from him than the old desire to have a cow for his own, to see her feeding in his garden, and his children drinking her milk, all came back upon him, and he hobbled after her as fast as he could go ; but such a wild-goose chase as she led him it is not worth while to describe. Through thistles, briers, and hedges, through woods and across meadows, and up and down hills, it seemed to Davy that he was being led to the end of the earth, and what was his surprise when toward nightfall, he found himself in the identical pasture field from which he had stolen the cow. If he had been afraid before, how much more was he afraid now !

He hid himself behind a stone-wall and waited for the night to fall, not daring even to lift up his head ; and when he saw the owner of the cows come to drive them home to be milked, he crouched down into the very earth.

All the cattle seemed delighted that the estray was come back among them, and gathered round her and licked her sides and her neck and her forehead, and made little moans as though they were talking and telling how glad they were.

"I shall never be able to divide her from her mates," thought Davy ; and his heart sank down within him; for, in spite of all he had suffered, he was fully resolved to steal the cow over again. Again fortune favored him. When the owner of the cattle drove the others out of the meadow, he turned this one, the handsomest of all, back, and Davy heard him say to her, "What business have you here? why don't you stay at home, you foolish creature?"

He could not quite tell what this meant; perhaps some one had bought the cow, and that thought made him doubly anxious to have her. So, just as soon as the gray twilight crept along the meadows, he tied the cow by the horn and led her away.

He was so weak by this time, with fasting, and the trouble he had had, that before he had travelled many miles he fell down, and could not go another step. He milked a little of the cow's milk in his hand, swallowed it, and then lay down to get a little further strength from sleep. But the sleep of a man who has stolen a cow is not refreshing, as you may well believe, and he arose in the morning chilled and cramped, and altogether in a worse condition than he had yet been.

He was obliged to halt so often during that day, that night again fell while he was yet a long way from home. So for the third night he lodged in the woods, and it is altogether probable that the crows and the squirrels talked to him just as they did before. Just as the sun was going down on the evening of the fourth day of his absence, he reached home and drove the cow in at the garden gate. His house was not burned down, as he had dreamed it was, but it was so changed that he hardly knew it. The front was all whitewashed, and there were curtains of scarlet stuff shining at the windows, and the grass had been clipt in the dooryard, some young trees set, and so many things done that Davy hardly knew it all for the same place.

All at once, while he yet stood amazed, his children came running out with shining faces and sleek hair, and began to cry, "O father, have you fetched her at last!" and then to fondle and caress the stolen cow as though she were an expected guest.

He had just got inside and had latched the gate, when turning round he saw his wife coming forth to meet him, if, indeed, that smiling woman dressed so neatly in a new gown and cap was his wife. "O Davy!" she cries, as she takes his hand and kisses it; "we began to be afraid the cow had run away with you!" And then she asks him as she leads him into the house, if he does n't think she has made a pretty good selection of a cow. Davy is so puzzled by all this that he does not know

what to say, and least of all does he know how
to look in his wife's face, for he sees plainly that,
however things are, she trusts him and believes
in him with all her heart. After a time the light
began to break in upon his brain. "Did you see
the rich man at the other end of the island?" she
says; and "O, isn't it a beautiful place?" and,
"Did he tell you how much I paid for the cow? I
thought I would come home and surprise you with
the good news; but good news travels fast, and when
I got home I found that you had already heard it,
and was gone to fetch her. How good it was of
you, to be sure!" And so she ran on till Davy understood it all. She had bought the identical cow
he had stolen, the morning before he reached the
rich man's meadows. He was no thief, after all,
and nobody in the world could ever know his secret. At first he felt very happy, and skipped and
danced about like a boy; but this could not last
with a wicked secret in his bosom, and he soon
began to droop and to lose all appetite, especially
for milk.

The house had been all brightened up inside as
well as out; and besides the scarlet curtains, there
was a new rag carpet and an easy-chair for himself, and a good many other things; but none nor
all of them could give him pleasure, for all the
time he knew himself to be a thief. One day his

wife said to him, "I thought, Davy, we were pre-
paring such a happy surprise for you, while you
were gone for the cow, but nothing seems to please
you, and we did it all for you!"

Then Davy broke down, and crying like a boy,
told his wife all the ugly truth; and after that he
had great pleasure in the new things, especially
the easy-chair, and milk tasted sweet to him, and
there was nowhere a happier family than that of
Davy Dreamer, for he was cured of his dreaming.

THE POTTER'S LUCK

I.

IT was the summer's prime, and all the court
    Were in the royal forest at their sport,
Hunting the hare to please the merry king,
Driving the game, and shooting on the wing;
Pages, and hounds, and troops of gentlemen
With horns that rung the echoes from the glen;
Ladies and lords with plumes and scarlet cloaks,
Sweeping across the shadows of the oaks.

II.

The while a potter, sitting by the way,
Took in his hand a little piece of clay,

And from the habit of his life began
To furbish it : he was a sad, sick man,
Having at home three children, pinched and pale, —
Is it a wonder that his heart should fail
With such a trouble tugging at the strings ?
This hunting pleasure of the merry king's
Was not for any man, as you will guess,
Being so friendly with his own distress ;
He knew not how to spend his holiday,
But just to keep on working with the clay !

III.

Well, as betwixt his palms the piece he rolled,
A little zigzag stone that shined like gold
Dropt out, and rested on his knee.   Just then
A lovely and sweet-hearted gentleman
Broke through the bushes, — leapt the wall that stood
About the outskirts of the royal wood,
And saw the potter sitting thus alone, —
Upon his knee the shining zigzag stone :
And in his white hand took it, paying down
On the poor potter's knee a silver crown ;
Then leapt the wall and through the bushes sped.
That night the potter came, with lightsome tread,
Home to his house, and when he showed the crown,
You would have thought the roof was coming down!
Such merry children it were good to see, —
One at his shoulder, one on either knee ;
And as a hand, brown as a leaf that's dead,
He laid upon each little golden head,

And told, with heart a-tremble in his tone,
About the shining bit of zigzag stone,
And all about the lovely gentleman,
Who, breaking through the bushes of the glen,
Leapt the great wall, and on his knee laid down —
The Lord knew why, he said — the silver crown,
His brown hands shook, his eyes with tears grew dim,
That such grand luck should fall by chance to him.

IV.

Then she, the eldest, at his shoulder, said,
Putting one fair, bare arm about his head,
Her eyes bent down, her fingers pale and thin,
Going so soft along his rough gray chin :
" You say the Lord knows why such luck should fall ;
It seems to me, now, just no luck at all !
But for your working all the day alone
Beside the royal wood, this precious stone
Would not have fallen upon your knee, — nor then
The silver crown of this fine gentleman !
To pay an honest debt is not so ill ;
To earn the pay you get, is better still ! "
And you who read the tale, I trust, agree
The honor went where honor ought to be.

A POET'S WALK.

ONCE his way a poet took
   Through a deep and dewy glen ;
Write about me in your book !
   Cried the redbreast, cried the wren.

Twittering low from every bush,
   Chirping loud from every tree,
Cried the pewet, cried the thrush,
   Cried the blackbird, write of me !

Sing about my eyes, my wings, —
   Mine is but a humble boon, —
So they cried, the silly things !
   Crossing each the other's tune.

But the poet, sign of grace
   Giving not by look or tone,
Turned into a shady place,
   Where a daisy lived alone.

All her modest shoulders hid
   In a veil of leaves of grass,
Dropping either snowy lid
   Sat she still to see him pass.

6

Then the poet, with a quill
　　That some eager bird had shook
Downward, all against her will,
　　Wrote about her in his book.

THE SNOW-FLOWER.

THE fields were all one field of snow,
　　The hedge was like a silver wall;
And when the March began to blow,
　　And clouds to fill, and rain to fall,
　　I wept that they should spoil it all.

At first the flakes with flurrying whirl
　　Hid from my eyes the rivulet,
Lying crooked, like a seam of pearl
　　Along some royal coverlet, —
　　I stood, as I remember yet,

With cheeks close-pressed against the pane,
　　And saw the hedge's hidden brown
Come out beneath the fretting rain;
　　And then I saw the wall go down, —
　　My silver wall, and all was brown.

And then, where all had been so white,
　　As still the rain slid slant and slow,

Bushes and briers came out in sight,
  And spikes of reeds began to show,
  And then the knot-grass, black and low.

One day, when March was at the close,
  The mild air balm, the sky serene,
The fields that had been fields of snows,
  And, after, withered wastes, were seen
  With here and there some tender green;

That day my heart came sudden up
  With pleasure that was almost pain, —
Being in the fields, I found a cup,
  Pure white, with just a blood-red vein
  Dashed round the edges, by the rain, —

The rain, which I that wild March hour
  So foolishly had wept to see,
Had shaped the snow into a flower,
  And thus had brought it back to me
  Sweeter than only snow could be.

EASY WORK.

LITTLE children, be not crying;
　　You have easy work to do;
Look not upward for the flying
　　Of the angels in the blue;

Look not for some great example,
　　Such as deaths of martyrs give;
One command above is ample
　　For the teaching you to live:

So that you will find out roses
　　Brighter than are by the brooks;
Poesy with sweeter closes
　　Than are in the poet's books;

Friends to gently watch and tend you
　　When your hours of pain go by,
And at last their prayers to lend you,
　　When your time has come to die.

In your working, in your praying,
　　In your actions, great or small,
In your hearts keep Jesus' saying, —
　　" Love each other ": this is all.

COURAGE.

KNOWING the right and true,
Let the world say to you
  Worst that it can :
Answer despite the blame,
Answer despite the shame,
I'll not belie my name, —
  I'll be a man !

Armed only with the right,
Standing alone to fight
  Wrong, old as time,
Holding up hands to God
Over the rack and rod, —
Over the crimson sod,
  That is sublime !

Monarchs of old, at will
Parcelled the world, but still
  Crowns may be won :
Yet there are piles to light, —
Putting all fear to flight,
Shouting for truth and right,
  Who will mount on ?

PART V.

THE CHARMED MONEY.

JERRY MASON had been hoeing two long hours in the garden; the earth was moist and black about the cabbages, the heavy gray leaves of which were lopping earthward to give their, as yet, soft hearts a better chance of maturing in the sun; the red seamy leaves of the beets testified to the good culture they had had, but as if they could not say it plainly enough, the beets themselves were come up half out of the ground to add their testimony, and the pale spiky tops of the onions stood up like soldiers in straight rows, saying, " Behold, there is not a weed among us." The tomatoes, bright with dew-drops and full of young fruit, gave out their pleasant odor most prodigally in payment for the care they had just received; and some few flowers, common to be sure, — but what flower is not beautiful ? — opened bright and honest in the sunshine, causing Jerry to leave his work for a moment, and, leaning on his hoe, contemplate their pinky and purple and yellow colors with an ecstasy of joy. He did not believe, for the moment, that the king's garden contained anything more de-

lightful than did his mother's. But even if that
were possible, he thought the king could not enjoy
its beauties half so much as he, because his pleasure was more than half derived from the fact that
himself had ploughed and sowed the garden, and
that the fruits and flowers before him were his, as
they could not have been if another than himself
had done the work. The eyes of the simple see
straight to the truth sometimes, when all the curious speculations of the wise are at fault, and I am
not sure but that Jerry was wise in feeling that
the king could not be so happy as he.

He did not think of his bare feet half buried in
the loose earth ; he did not think of his patched
trousers, and that his shirt was not linen in the
wristbands and collar even ; and for a minute, at
least, he did not think how hot the sun was shining down upon him, and how tired he was.

"Jerry !" called his mother, leaning from the
low window of her little house, — "Jerry, my child,
you may as well go and feed the old sitting goose,
and the change of work will rest you."

"Yes, mother," answered Jerry ; and as he took
off his hat and wiped his face, he looked across the
field where Henry Gordon was idly flying his kite,
and almost envied him : he was a rich man's son,
and neither had to hoe nor to feed an old goose.

But Jerry was too good, and too happy, for the

most part, to envy any one long, and directly, hanging his hoe in the fork of a tree that stood by the garden gate, he prepared the accustomed food, crossed the barn-yard where the hens were cackling and picking the grains from the chaff that was scattered about, passed along the field where the cow was nibbling the short grass, went over the brook on a bridge of stones he had built the last summer, climbed the slope beyond, and suddenly stood still. The old goose sitting in the hollow of a black stump close by was protruding her neck, flopping her wings, and hissing at a terrible rate. "You are crazy, ain't you, you ugly old goose!" exclaimed Jerry, raising up and clinching one hand as if he would hit her if he had anything with which to do it. "Do you think I am afraid of you? Why I have milked our cow on the wrong side, been all the way to mill for mother, and besides that, have killed two garter-snakes,— one of them half a yard long and striped and checked like a ribbon — Shut up your wings, you old — whew!" and Jerry climbed to the top of a neighboring stump and shouted at the top of his voice, — cutting circles in the air with his hat, and beckoning with his hand in great earnestness. Farmer Hix stopped his team in the adjoining field and listened, thinking Jerry was shouting for help. Mrs. Mason put her head out of the back door; she, too, had heard

Jerry, and feared some bad accident had happened. A moment the farmer stood still, his horses turning their heads in the direction of the call, and the mother leaned and listened in trembling anxiety; but the door closed presently, and the farmer ploughed on again: both had heard Jerry say to Henry Gordon, who was seen running with his kite across the field, "Don't you think, our old goose has got goslings!"

That was enough to make any boy climb to the top of a stump and shout for joy, Jerry thought. How many she had he did not know, but he would not be surprised to find that every egg was hatched, — three of the golden little creatures he saw, he is sure, and if the old goose would only come off the nest he could soon tell; he would dare get a stick and drive her off, but he thinks he won't.

"What is it! what is it!" cries Henry Gordon, running as fast as he can, and quite regardless of the kite that drags along the ground as he runs. "What is it! have you found a bag of gold?"

He is older by two or three years than Jerry, and wears much finer clothes, but he is not a finer looking boy, for all that. His boots are of the finest leather, and polished very bright, — brighter than Jerry's best ones, which he only wears of Sundays, which hang over a peg at the head of his bed in his mother's garret; and his hat is so fresh and new, and the ends of the green ribbon tied around it flutter so gayly, that Jerry is abashed for a moment, and says he fears Henry will not be paid for having run so fast, and especially if he has spoiled his fine kite into the bargain; that he has not anything worth showing, — some little goslings, that is all. But Henry has never seen a gosling, for it is only lately that he has come from a great city; and he says the old kite is of no value, he can get as many better ones as he pleases; he rather hopes it is spoiled, and so by its string he winds it up to him, and, tossing it at the feet of Jerry, bestows it on him in a patronizing sort of way that would have offended him if he had not felt in his heart that he was equal to any boy anywhere.

When the goose had been fed, and the goslings too, Jerry showed his new friend the stone bridge across the brook, which bridge, both concluded, might be greatly beautified and improved if they would unite their strength and ingenuity and give a day to the work. He showed him his mother's cow, and assured him that he dare plat her tail together, count the rings on her horns, or even go up to her on the " wrong side "!

Then they went to the cow-shed where the straw was in which the hens made their nests, and after this to the garden, where Henry pulled some of the finest flowers for his little neighbor. When it was dinner-time and Jerry's mother called him, his young friend went into the house with him, and partook, with great relish, of the simple meal that was spread.

When he went away he invited Jerry to come to his house and ride his horse, and go gunning with him, which Jerry felt would be a great delight to him to do, and which he afterward did many times; for from that day Henry and Jerry were excellent friends, working and playing together a great deal. The rich man's son soon lost a good deal of the foolish pretension he had at first, and what he did not lose Jerry readily forgave. Sometimes, indeed, he would throw off his coat and strip away shoes and stockings, and enter with hearty good-will into whatever was to be done. They went together to the same school, for there was but one in the neighborhood, and once or twice had hats and jackets alike. They gathered nuts together, and berries; made hay together, and picked apples; shouted, and sung, and made whistles, and drove the cows home one with another. Then, too, O idle dreaming! they made plans for the years to come, — plans of what they would do when they were men. They would always be neighbors, and divide whatever they had, just as they did their goslings and hollyhocks now.

" Why don't you come to see my mother ? "
said Henry often to Mrs. Mason, for he could not
see why the mothers of such friends should not be
friends too.   And Mrs. Mason always said she
would like to do so if she could get time, but somehow it happened that she never did find time, and
never went.   Mrs. Gordon rode in her fine carriage
to a fine church on Sundays, and wore a silk gown
and her hair in curls.   Mrs. Mason put her hair
plainly under a plain cap, and walked across the
meadow to the school-house to attend service.   Mrs.
Gordon dined sumptuously at five, Mrs. Mason
simply at twelve ; one lived in a big house and was
served by a good many maids and men, the other
in a very small house serving herself ; the one saw
the sun shine through a lace curtain, and the other
through rose-vines.   So it was that Mrs. Gordon
said, " Thank you, my dear, it will give me the
greatest pleasure when I have an hour to spare,"
in answer to Jerry's invitation of, " You must
come and see my mother."   And so it happened
that she never found an hour to spare, and never
went to see Jerry's mother.

Three years went by of the closest friendship between the lads, and all this time they did not understand exactly why their mothers could not find
time to visit each other.   It was the greatest pleasure to Henry to go with bare feet across the nicely

scoured floor of Mrs. Mason, and to sit with her
and Jerry, where the roses looked in at the window, and partake of her home-made cakes and
bread, and eat her preserved fruits, which were
never so good at home; the wind came in so fresh
and sweet from the hay-field beyond the hollow,
and the birds made such music in the garden, and
Mrs. Mason had such a sweet voice and a pleasant
way, his mother would be delighted, he was sure,
if she could only find time to come to the cottage.

Mrs. Mason sat by the fire waiting for Jerry,
who had gone to carry a fine yellow pumpkin of
his own raising to Henry's mother, that Henry
might have some just such pies as he was to have,
— sat rocking and musing before the bright wood-
fire, wishing somebody would come in and cheer
the lonesomeness a little, for the night was falling
and the snow lay cold and smooth everywhere, far
as she could see. The straw-roofed shed of the
cow was beautified like a queen's chamber. No
king could put such a roof on his house as the
snow had put on that. The fences seemed made
of pieces of snow, the trees to be trees of snow,
and all so still and cold. The cock went early to
bed, fluttering the white shower from the limb of
the tree that lodged him, — fluttering it down as
though he did not care for it at all, and turning his
bright eyes to his mates that sat beside him, sober

and uncomfortable enough. He was rather glad, for his part, that so cold and snowy a night was come; it brought out his gallantry and his fortitude. But generally the aspect of things without, in spite of all the beauty, was cheerless. The tea, in the old teapot cracked and bound with hoops of tin, had been simmering a good while, the fire began to make a little red light on the snow beneath the window, and a candle to be needed in the dim room where Jerry's mother sat, when she heard the creaking of the gate, and, rising, looked out of the window. It was growing quite dusky; and though she saw two boys coming toward the door, she could not at first believe it was Jerry and Henry, so quietly they came, arm in arm, and talking so low and so earnestly. What could it mean? Of all times this was the one to make them merry, for there is more exhilaration in snow than in wine, and birds and boys are alike fond of dipping into it, and chirping and chattering when it lies over the ground loose and white. Close came the young friends past rose-bushes and lilacs all wrapped so prettily, and never once did they turn to look or dash the white weights from the bending twigs. Nor did they step aside from the open path and break their way, ploughing off snow-furrows as they came, as boys love to do. No merry voices rang through the clear silence; but soberly and straightforward they came, as if the snow had buried beneath it some great joy.

And so, indeed, it had. They were about to be separated for a long, long while. It had been decided at home that Henry should go away to a military school, not to come home for six months, or it might be for a year.

Jerry's mother was sad enough when she heard the news ; and to keep the moisture from gathering to drops in her eyes, she rubbed the tin hoops of her blue teapot with the towel, till they shone again.

Henry said he was sorry he was to go ; but for all of his saying so, he was not as sorry as Jerry was. He had new boots and a new coat and hat, and a number of other things of which he was fully conscious all the while. Then, too, he would write every day, and it would be almost the same as seeing him, and he would come home often, for Henry had been used to having his own way, and could not think but that his will would still be his law, as it always had been.

The next day Jerry climbed to the top of the gate-post, and watched the carriage that took Henry from him drive away. Through tears he caught a glimpse of his little friend, but his little friend did not once look toward him.

That was Jerry's first sorrow. No number of

yellow goslings could have brought the old light into his red eyes that morning; no pinks nor daffodils, though the garden had been full of them, could have seemed to him bright as the smile of his playmate.

A letter was promised him by the first mail; and all the interval seemed to Jerry a blank, a time of nothing, that he would be glad to push right along and have done with. It would not be seeing his friend, but it would be something; it would be a great thing: he had never received a letter in his life, sealed and meant all for him. He wondered how it would begin and how it would end, and what, in fact, his friend would say, and how he would say it. One thing would be in it, that he knew, that Henry was very lonesome and wanted to see him so bad. That would be in the letter, and he was not sure but that it would be in it a great many times; indeed, it was not unlikely the entire letter would be made up of love for him and anxiety to see him. Henry knew so much and would have learned so much, even in three days, at a military school, that he supposed the letter would be a model, — and what an advantage to him to have such a fine friend!

And at last the day on which the mail was expected was come, and at last it went by and was time to go to the post-office, two miles from his

mother's house. The snow was deep and it was
cold after sunset, but little cared Jerry for that ;
he would run because he could not help it, and
that would keep him warm ; and, besides, if a boy
thought much of a boy and wrote him so, he would
feel bad to know a boy did not think enough of a
boy to go after the letter, because it was a little
cold. So buttoning the old coat that was outgrown
and a good deal worn, Jerry set out, never minding the still air that almost cut his face, as if it
tried to thrust him back into the warm house,
never minding the white, cold glimmer of the stars
that seemed to say, " It's no use," never minding
anything, because he was a boy that liked a boy,
and supposed a boy liked him back just as well.
He was not long in walking the two miles. He
did not once think he might have gone faster and
with more comfort if Mrs. Gordon had offered
him Henry's pony to ride, when she asked him
to bring her letters. He did not think of anything but the pleasure he would have in breaking
the seal and reading to his mother every word
Henry wrote. The two miles were a good deal
longer when Jerry went home, not because he was
going home, and not because it was more up hill ;
it was a good deal colder, too, and his coat seemed
thinner ; it nearly froze his hand to carry the bun-
dle of letters and papers for Mrs. Gordon, and the

sharp wind brought the water to his eyes, — he
had no letter from Henry. An ugly distrust came
into his heart as he went along, — the moon might
drop right down out of the sky, for all he knew,
and he hardly thought it unlikely that his mother
should have set fire to the house and run away
while he was gone. If it was possible that Henry
could have broken his " word and honor," his
" double word and honor," what might not be possible ?

Henry was not sick, for there, in a fair, firm hand,
was a letter to his parents.

He could not stop and ask Mrs. Gordon if Henry
were well; something choked him, and he must go
home.

An hour he sat on a stool in the corner and
cried, in spite of all his mother could say to
soothe him; but at last when she told him to
wipe his eyes and run over to Mrs. Gordon's and
see what was in Henry's letter, he stifled his sobs
and obeyed.

Mrs. Gordon looked up from her reading as Jerry came in, in a way that said plainly she was surprised and annoyed; and when little Fanny Gordon
ran from listening at her mother's knee and offered
Jerry a chair at the fireside, she shook her head at
the little girl, and whispered something which Jerry thought meant she must not ask him to sit

down. Fanny half hid her face in her mother's lap; but she turned her eyes full of tears and sweet pity toward Jerry, and the frown of the mother lost its power on him, and for a moment he scarcely cared whether Henry had said anything about him or not.

Every mail day all the winter, whether it were gusty or mild, freezing or thawing, Jerry went regularly to the post-office, but there was never any letter for him. Once little Fanny had spoken to him through the fence, and told him that her brother Henry had written to know what he was doing now-a-days, and said that he should write to him as soon as he found time. She said, too, that when she went away to school, as she was to do in the spring, she would write a letter to him, and she would not tell her mother nor anybody else what she wrote.

After this Jerry tried to make excuses for Henry, — he was very busy, no doubt, and had as many letters to write home as he could find time to do; and as he worked, spading the garden, he often tried to work out a letter in his brain. But he could not tell very well how to begin, nor how to end, nor what to say, — a boy in a military school might not feel much like a boy spading in his mother's garden.

The old goose brought out her troop of young

goslings again; the flowers all looked over the garden fence toward "Fanny's house," as Jerry fancied; the heads of the cabbages were hardening, and their great gray leaves lopping toward the ground again. Jerry could not go to school now as he used to do when he was smaller, but had to stay at home and work. Fanny was gone away to school now, and had kept her promise and written a letter to Jerry, — a very little letter made up of very little sentences, and with a superscription that made three very crooked lines all across and across the envelope. To Jerry's thinking, however, there never was a much better letter written. All the time he kept it in his pocket, reading it again and again as often as he found leisure, though he knew every word from first to last. He could not bear to put it away with his few books; it seemed like a free ticket to the good-will of everybody; so he kept it, as I said, all the time in his pocket. He found the distrust that he had had in his heart since Henry went away growing rapidly less, and now and then he suspected that he had been very wicked in imagining the moon could fall, or his mother burn up the house and run away. Suddenly he stopped from his working, tired, but looking well pleased; he had been very industrious and done a full day's work, though it wanted yet three hours of night. He had made up his mind to

write to Henry ; for since Fanny had written him,
" I am very well ; I hope you are very well. I
don't like here so well as home. Do your goslings grow ? Have you heard from Henry ?" he
had felt that everybody he knew liked him, and
would be glad to know how well he was doing.
So the happiness he thought he should give to
another was all bright in his face as he hung his
hoe in the pear-tree, and breaking three cabbage-
leaves, not crooked and deep green, but fair and
gray with bloom, made his way to the brookside,
where the shadow of a maple lay thick and cool,
and near where the stone bridge caused the water
to stop and make some silver talk before it went
over.

From the cherry-tree by the door he had brought
some little withes, and having sharpened them with
his teeth, began the composition of a letter, — using
his hat-crown for a desk, the cabbage-leaves for
paper, and the twigs for pens. Never was poet
wrapped more happily in a dream than he in his
work, when all at once he became conscious of
footsteps and heard a voice, not unfamiliar, except
in its derision, say, " Ha, boy ! I say you ought to
take out a patent for that sort of paper : how are
you, though ? " Jerry's senses were a good deal
bewildered, and he could not believe at first it was
Henry Gordon who stood before him, resting his

THE CHARMED MONEY.

polished gun on the ground, holding a cigar in one
hand, and surveying him with such cool indifference.

He tried to rise and return civilly the rude salu-
tation of the young cadet; and as he advanced he
saw that Henry was not alone, but accompanied
by a youth whom he introduced as a classmate,
naming Jerry as a boy he used to know; asking
Jerry how things were getting on in *his* line, and
saying that, as regarded himself, he hoped his soul
had got a little above potatoes during his absence.
He did not speak even of Jerry's mother, who had
done him so many favors; and to complete the insult, he tossed at Jerry, as he passed along, a small
piece of money, saying, " Take that, boy, and buy
you a copy-book and a pen or two."

Jerry did not speak; he felt as if he could never
speak again; he could hardly persuade himself
that it was indeed Henry Gordon who had stood
but now before him, and as long as he could see
gazed the way he was going. The very buttons of
his coat seemed to mock him with their shining;
and there lay the money on the ground at his feet,
and the cabbage-leaves wilting in the sun, for
where the shadow had been an hour ago the sun
shone hot enough now.

All the world was changed, and it seemed for a
little while not only possible, but highly probable,

that his mother might set fire to the house and run away, and the moon drop out of the sky ; if anything could stay back such events, it would be the letter from Fanny. He put his hand in his pocket, to be sure that it was still there ; and, stooping, picked up the piece of money and placed it in the opposite pocket, to keep balance. Fanny's letter should teach him the world was not all bad ; that piece of money, that it was not all good. In itself it was but a harmless piece of money, and he would not have known it from a thousand others, but it had been in contact with the hand that shrunk away from him ; it had been flung at him in charity, — at him a boy as good as any other boy, as honest and as honorable. In all respects he was not Henry's equal, to be sure, but he would set to work that very day and make himself so. If he had not had Henry's advantages, neither had Henry had his ! And straight he set out for home. His heart misgave him almost when he reached the door and saw the tea-table spread in holiday style, and for three. Mrs. Mason had learned that Henry was come home, and was thinking what a pleasant time they would all have once more. It was hard to tell his good dear mother that he had already seen Henry, and how he had seen him. More than once, as they sat together, Jerry's mother arose from the table to attend some little duty, she said, but in truth it was to dry her eyes; and more than once Jerry said he did not care what Henry Gordon thought of him; but his mother knew it was because he cared a great deal that he said so.

Already his mind was stung into activity, and a development was going on, of which he was not himself aware.

Years of persevering endeavor, of hard work with the hands and harder with the brain, we pass by, — years in which hope has been busy with him, so busy that he has felt the steep way they have climbed together less toilsome. Teachers and schools have not been accessible to him much, except, indeed, the common school of humanity and the great teacher, God, in his works. These works he has read and reread; these he has studied, and he has studied himself, and his duties to himself and his fellows. He feels the nobility of true and honest manhood, afraid of nothing but doing wrong, ambitious of nothing but coining the ability with which he has been endowed to right use. For he is not ambitious to serve the world nor the state, — measured against such great requirements he feels unequal; he is content with making even a little spot of earth greener for his having lived; he thinks it something of an achievement to turn weeds into good rich soil, and make wheat or roses grow where, but for him, barrenness would have been. He does not believe he could have made himself a poet if he had mortised rhymes together never so ingeniously ; nor does he suppose he could manage the affairs of nations, because he can manage a plough. Nevertheless, he is a proud man, — proud of his cleared land and of his woodland, — proud of his brooks and of his cows, — of his harvests and of his garden, — of his beautiful cottage, — of the vines about the porch and of the well-bound volumes that shine row over row against the wall, — of his mother, sitting beside him so comfortable and so respectable, — proud that he owes no man anything, and proud that he is not proud in any mean and selfish sense.

A thousand times he might have resented the old insult of the piece of money, but he feels that " time at last sets all things even," and he is quite contented to wait, — so well content, indeed, that there is no waiting to do. He could not have been so well avenged any way as he is by his indifference.

It is the middle of June, and the garden is full of flowers that still look toward Mrs. Gordon's a good deal, though Jerry says he don't care which way they look ; but we are quite sure they would not be so many nor so bright if there were no bright eyes looking down upon them from the opposite windows. There are bright flowers immediately under the windows where the bright eyes are gazing forth so often ; but to those eyes the flowers in the distance show the best.

Fanny is a woman now, and though she sends no more letters to her friend Jerry that no one knows anything of, she sends a great many glances as full of kindly meaning as were the little sentences sent him so long ago. She has been home from school a whole year ; and though many times, in her walks and drives, she has met Jerry, and smiled upon him very sweetly, he has returned her smiles with only formal politeness. Of course Fanny Gordon does not care much for the like of him, — that is what he says to himself, and so he keeps up a show of indifference that he is very far from feeling.

Henry has been at home a long time, too, spending his time in idleness and in worse than idleness, so rumor says, and that things are growing from bad to worse with the Gordons. Still they manage to keep up an outside show, and hold their heads much above working-people like the Masons. But when the foundation is undermined, the time will come that the house must fall, and that time came to the Gordons.

It was early autumn ; there was a little fire on the hearth, but the door toward the flower-garden stood open, and Jerry sat in the door watching the moonlight as it played along the grass and shone among the stalks of such of the hardier blossoms as yet remained.

All at once his heart gave a little start, — was it some bird rustling among the dry leaves? No, it was the step of Fanny rustling along the fallen leaves. She came without hesitation, without blushing, straight to where Jerry was sitting. "I could not go away," she said, putting out her hand to him, "without first coming to bid your mother and you good by!"

"Go away, Fanny! Where are you going, and why?" cried Jerry, surprised into cordiality and earnestness.

Then Fanny sat down beside him in the moonlight and told him where she was going, and why. "Our fortune is all gone, and somebody must do something," she concluded.

"But why should you go away to do something?"

"Because," Fanny answered, "we have no friends here!" and then her voice first faltered, and she hid her face in her hands.

"No friends!" said Jerry; "with my mother and myself here? O Fanny, how can you say that?"

Then she told him that she was sure there was

no reason why himself and his mother should be their friends; but at any rate, they had no others, and she was going away to teach school, or to learn to sew, or to do something by which she could take care of herself. "Just think, Jerry," she says, "I have not a glove to my hand!" And she held out her hand to him, red as a rose with the evening chill.

Jerry took it between both his. "And suppose, Fanny, I should always keep it this way," he said, "you would not need a glove, would you?"

Fanny's face was all bright with blushes when Mrs. Mason came to say that supper was ready; and the place she took at the table that night became hers for all her life before long; for, of course, she and Jerry were married, and two birds were never happier under the mother's wing than were they with the mother of Jerry. Everything prospered with them, and by and by they were the rich people in the town where they lived, and not the Gordons at all.

One dreary night, when the outside show could not be kept up any longer, when they were in fact reduced to the last sixpence, they sat together, Mrs. Gordon and her son Henry, lamenting their hard fortune, and blaming each other, and blaming Fanny, whom they had never been to visit, and blaming everything but their own foolish pride and

7 *

perverseness for the ruin and degradation that was now impending.

Both started at the sound of a footstep; it was a creditor's, no doubt.

"What brought you here? I don't owe you anything!" exclaimed Henry, sullenly, when he saw that the visitor was Jerry Mason.

"No," replied Jerry, "but I owe you a great deal"; and taking from his pocket the piece of money Harry had flung at him so long ago, he laid it down on the table before him. Henry trembled and blushed for shame; but when Jerry took his hand and said, "This piece of money has been a charm that has kept me from idleness and uselessness; it has added to my lands and built me a house, beautified my garden, clothed my mother, and made her old age happy and respectable, developed my own manhood, and crowned me with the love of the best of women. For all this I owe you something, and I am come to pay you. Take first this money and see what it can do for you. You are yet in the prime of life and can retrieve and achieve everything; come with me with as hearty a good-will as you came to look at my goslings, and we will devise the way." Henry took the hand extended to him, and brushing the tears from his eyes, — the first ones that had wet them for long years, — said in accents that trembled, "I will go, Jerry, if you think I am worth saving; and my mother shall go too. Come, mother!" So all three went together, and Fanny met and embraced them; and then they sat down together and made plans for the future, and that was the happiest night of their lives.

TO A STAGNANT POND.

O POND of the meadow,
    So low and so black,
Say why are you lying thus,
    Flat on your back!

Week in and week out,
    And from night until morn,
You have been doing nothing
    Since first you were born.

Now if you are not dead,
    But only just dumb,
Get up, sir, and take off
    Your jacket of scum!

No sweet little flower
    To your dull bosom bends;

You have only the hop-toad
    And snake for your friends!

No bird to your dark wave
    Comes twittering down,
And the grass all about you
    Is withered and brown.

It is time, and high time,
    You were setting to work,
You sordid, unlovable,
    Beggarly shirk!

Just think, with your brow
    Into black wrinkles curled,
You never have gladdened
    A heart in the world!

And if you would henceforth
    Escape from abuse,
Get up, I beseech you,
    And be of some use!

Close at hand, only hid by
    The sheep-grazing hill,
Your gad-about sister
    Is turning a mill.

Her path is so pleasant,
    Her smile is so bright,
The flocks stay about her
    All day and all night.

The wild mint leans lowly,
  Her kiss is so sweet,
And the stones that she treads on
  Sing under her feet.

With foam-flowers always
  Her wet locks are crowned,
And her bushes with berries
  Blush all the year round.

She counts not the mill-work
  As doing her wrong,
But makes the wheel partner,
  And dances along.

And so, with her life
  And her labor content,
She is queen of the meadow
  By common consent.

Now here is a secret,
  Receive it in faith, —
True life is in action,
  Stagnation is death.

And this you may learn
  From your sister, the brook,
As though it were written
  And bound in a book.

You die in your torpor,
    She rests in her strife,
Because she is keeping
    The law of her life.

And would you be happy
    As she at her mill,
Throw off your scum jacket,
    And work with a will.

THE POET TO THE PAINTER.

PAINTER, paint me a sycamore,
    A spreading and snowy-limbed tree,
    Making cool shelter for three,
And like a green quilt at the door
    Of the cabin near the tree,
    Picture the grass for me,
With a winding and dusty road before,
    Not far from the group of three,
    And the silver sycamore-tree.

'T will take your finest skill to draw
    From that happy group of three,
    Under the sycamore-tree,
The little girl in the hat of straw
And the faded frock, for she

Is as fair as fair can be.
You have painted frock and hat complete!
Now the color of snow you must paint her feet;
Her cheeks and lips from a strawberry-bed;
From sunflower-fringes her shining head.

Now, painter, paint the hop-vine swing
   Close to the group of three,
And a bird with bright brown eyes and wing,
   Chirping merrily.
   "Twit twit, twit twit, twee!"
That is all the song he makes,
And the child to mocking laughter breaks.
   Answering, "Here are we,
   Father and mother and me!"
Pretty darling, her world is small, —
Father and mother and she are all.

Ah, painter, your hand is still!
   You have made the group of three
   Under the sycamore-tree,
But you cannot make all the skill
   Of your colors say, "Twit twit, twee!"
   Nor the answering, "Here are we,
   Father and mother and me."
I'll be a poet, and paint with words
Talking children and chirping birds.

ONLY A DREAM.

"The flighty purpose never is o'ertook,
Unless the deed go with it."

ONE time, when lying in my bed,
   Many a night ago,
Flying and flapping over my head,
   There went a cunning crow.
I might have struck the creature dead,
   She sailed so near and slow.

I might have struck her as she went,
   (All in a dream lay I,)
But thought was on the method bent,
   My fated bird should die;
And when at last the shaft was sent,
   The archer's time was by.

" O cruel, cunning bird," I said,
   " What made you fly away?
I would have dyed your black wings red,
   With but a moment's stay.
Then you had flown without your head, " —
   (All in a dream I lay.)

Her nest was in a giant tree,
   So safe and snug and high;
And I said, " If there your young ones be,
   I 'll kill them when they fly."

'T was hard just then to climb and see, —
   (All in a dream lay I.)

Afield with my two boys one morn,
   (This was the vision's close,)
Each with a basket full of corn
   To plant the furrowed rows;
Right over us, in full-fledged scorn,
   There went three wicked crows.

"You might have killed us once," they cried,
   "Our mother's nest you knew;
But now our wings are strong and wide,
   And we can caw at you!"
Then vanished all my manhood's pride, —
   The birds had spoken true.

"O father," said my boys to me,
   "'T is plain that crows will lie;
You knew what they would grow to be,
   Before they learned to fly,
And would have killed them in the tree," —
   (All in a dream lay I.)

Many and many a night since then
   I 've called to mind that crow,
And thought how many thousand men
   Through all their lifetime go,
Planning out times and seasons when
   They will do thus and so;

But all their joys are shallow joys,
  Their praise augments their woes;
For I remember when my boys
  Denounced the taunting crows,
A voice inside of all their noise,
  Condemning me, arose.

INVENTORY OF A DRUNKARD.

A HUT of logs without a door,
  Minus a roof and ditto floor ;
A clapboard cupboard without crocks,
Nine children without shoes or frocks;
A wife that has not any bonnet
With ribbon bows and strings upon it,
Scolding and wishing to be dead,
Because she has not any bread.

A teakettle without a spout,
A meat-cask with the bottom out,
A " comfort " with the cotton gone,
And not a bed to put it on.
A handle without any axe,
A hatchel without wool or flax ;
A potlid and a wagon-hub,
And two ears of a washing-tub ;
Three broken plates of different kinds,
Some mackerel tails and bacon-rinds ;

A table without leaves or legs,
One chair, and half a dozen pegs,
One oaken keg with hoops of brass,
One tumbler of dark-green glass ;
A fiddle without any strings,
A gunstock, and two turkey wings.

O readers of this inventory,
Take warning by its graphic story ;
For little any man expects,
Who wears good shirts with buttons in 'em,
Ever to put on cotton checks,
And only have brass pins to pin 'em !
'T is, remember, little stitches
Keep the rent from growing great ;
When you can't tell beds from ditches,
Warning words will be too late.

HUNTER'S SONG.

I KNOW a mountain high,
  With its head against the sky,
Where the stormy eagles fly
    East and west ;
There, at morning's ruddy gleam,
And in evening's purple beam,
I have heard the nursling scream
    From the nest !

O, I love that mountain high,
With its head against the sky,
And the hungry nurslings' cry,
    All forlorn ;
For as winds went to and fro,
Cutting furrows through the snow,
In a hunter's hut so low,
    I was born.

O, I love the rocky glade,
Where my little brothers played,
Where together they are laid
    In green beds ;
With a water murmuring nigh
Its eternal lullaby,
And a blue strip of the sky
    At their heads.

HAGEN WALDER.

THE day with a cold, dead color
    Was rising over the hill,
When little Hagen Walder
    Went out to grind in th' mill.

All vainly the light in zigzags
    Fell through the frozen leaves,
And like a broidery of gold
    Shone on his ragged sleeves.

No mother had he to brighten
   His cheek with a kiss, and say,
" 'T is cold for my little Hagen
   To grind in the mill to-day."

And that was why the north-winds
   Seemed all in his path to meet,
And why the stones were so cruel
   And sharp beneath his feet.

And that was why he hid his face
   So oft, despite his will,
Against the necks of the oxen
   That turned the wheel in th' mill.

And that was why the tear-drops
   So oft did fall and stand
Upon their silken coats that were
   As white as a lady's hand.

So little Hagen Walder
   Looked at the sea and th' sky,
And wished that he were a salmon
   In the silver waves to lie ;

And wished that he were an eagle,
   Away through th' air to soar,
Where never the groaning mill-wheel
   Might vex him any more ;

And wished that he were a pirate,
  To burn some cottage down,
And warm himself; or that he were
  A market-lad in the town,

With bowls of bright, red strawberries
  Shining on his stall,
And that some gentle maiden
  Would come and buy them all.

So little Hagen Walder
  Passed, as the story says,
Through dreams, as through a golden gate,
  Into realities.

And when the years changed places,
  Like the billows, bright and still,
In th' ocean, Hagen Walder
  Was the master of the mill.

And all his bowls of strawberries
  Were not so fine a show
As are his boys and girls at church,
  Sitting in a row.

A GOOSE AND A CROW.

TWO geese, scarcely knowing
  The east from the west,
Got on to the water
  And rode off abreast, —
Geese, you know, are not famed
  For their wisdom, at best.

Well, these were perhaps
  Neither greater nor less
Than their fellows, — each had on
  A very white dress,
And both had short tails,
  And a neck like an S.

The morning was genial,
  The water was still,
And each with her heart
  On the end of her bill
Began telling secrets,
  As geese sometimes will.

" All ganders are vulgar,"
  One said, " all so low
That one can't respect them;
  My dear, do you know
I am really going
  To marry a crow ! "

"A crow!" cried the other one,
    Slanting her eye :
"What! one of those black things
    That swim in the sky?
How strange it would be
    To go swimming so high!

"But are you sure, darling,
    (Though 't is n't for me
To question your wisdom,)
    That you shall agree?
I 've heard say that crows
    Have their nests in a tree!"

"And what if they do, dear?
    Should that make you doubt
My wisdom?"   "No, darling,
    My fears were about
The poor little goslings, —
    Might they not fall out?"

"Fall out of their own nest
    Ah, where could you go
To find such a foolish fear?
    Do you not know
That the carefullest bird
    In the world is the crow?

"And when he shall have young
    To quicken his care,

Do you think he will leave his nest
  Out of repair?
Or, pray, do you think that
  A crow is a bear?

" Why, only this morning,
  The one I propose
To marry (be sure,
  He's the kindest of crows)
Assured me that I should do
  Just as I chose!

" And so if I don't like
  My nest in a tree,
Inasmuch as he means
  To defer thus to me,
I will come down and build
  On the ground."   " If that he

" Continue his deference
  When you are matched,"
Said the wiser goose, " and if when
  Discords are hatched,
He shall have no sharp claws
  Nor your eyes to be scratched! "

" I see," said the first goose,
  Receiving amiss
The warning, " that you, madam,
  Envy my bliss, —
8

Good morning." The last word
   Was almost a hiss.

They married, this stranger pair,
   For better or worse,
And, being opposed
   In their natures, of course,
They quarrelled, — she left him,
   Brought suit for divorce, —

And charged him with saying
   A goose was a goose,
Also with most cruel
   Neglect and abuse,
And with being black, — all true,
   But no sort of use !

And so they are living, —
   He high in his tree,
Misanthropic as ever
   A crow was, and she
Decrying the courts
   That won't grant a decree.

He says to his friends
   He was not understood, —
Says he would n't get married
   Again if he could ;
And she says he lies,
   For he knows that he would.

PART VI.

THE MAN WITH A STONE IN HIS HEART.

ONCE, in the suburb of a beautiful village, which in our story we will call Heatherford, there lived an old woman whose only wealth was her garden and her little son Elijah, or Ligie, for that was the pet name which the fond mother gave her boy. No cottage in all the village was brighter and prettier with pots of flowers and tidy keeping than that belonging to Ligie's mother. Indeed, it was no unfrequent thing to see rich people stop their carriages and look into the garden, where the finely cultivated vegetables looked almost as well as the flowers that fringed the beds where they grew. At the foot of the garden, which sloped to the south, a spring broke out of a green wall of grass, and, escaping from the shadow of a willow-tree that grew there, ran crookedly away, shining and laughing as far as you could see. No corn had blades so thick and so green as that which Ligie planted and hoed, and no poppies were so large and so red as those fringing his cornfield.

Sometimes after sunset Ligie's mother might be

seen walking down the clean paths between the lady-slippers and the lilacs, talking to her child in a voice low and soft, and at other times gathering rose-leaves or hops in her white apron, scaring the birds that went early to bed, and making them sing their good-night songs anew. When the dew came there was contention between the rose-bushes and the hop-vines as to which smelled the sweeter, and Ligie and his mother, as they went up and down the paths, could never decide it; the bees loved the roses best, but the birds swung on the hop-vines, and sung in the hop-vines the oftenest.

Often Ligie's mother praised the industry and skill of her little son; but she loved him more than the beautiful garden. It is probable that the people who admired the blossoming bean-vines and the waving corn saw only in Ligie a homely little gardener; but to his mother no marigold was so bright as his head, and no violet so blue as his eyes, and the spring-water running away in sunshine was to her music less pleasant than his laughter.

As Ligie grew older, however, it was less and less often she heard this pleasant music; for the boy grew silent and thoughtful, and, pitiful to relate, more and more discontented, — sometimes, indeed, he would forget the work, and wander away to the ends of the earth in dreams.

Every day the garden seemed narrower, and every day his thoughts flew higher and more discontentedly away. Grass was seen to grow in places from which it had been carefully kept in former times, the raspberry-vines to lop untied, and the strawberries to blush more and more faintly, as Ligie bent over them less and less often.

Many a time he leaned on his hoe-handle, and, gazing wistfully — I am afraid enviously — after some gay equipage, wished himself anywhere away from his mother's little garden, and out of sight of her poor little house. He wished there were no gardens in the world, sometimes, and sometimes that he might wake up in the morning and find his pillow a pillow all of gold; for he thought idleness and money were the greatest blessings that could come to anybody, and desired most of all things to wear fine clothes, and to ride horses that were sleek and galloped over the country fleet as the wind.

" My dear son is sick," thought the good mother of the discontented boy, and she gave him time and times to rest from his work, and baked cakes for him, and made him soft beds, and kissed 'and petted him very tenderly. But Ligie had been always used to her loving care, and received it as he did the air and the other common blessings of his life.

One day, when the customary meal of bread and milk was set before him, he went away from the table without so much as breaking the bread; he said to his mother he was sick, but in his heart he thought if he could not have meat and honey he would not eat at all. Discontented with his mother, with himself, and with everything, he cast himself on the ground by the spring beneath the willow; but the murmur of the waters could not silence the murmur in his heart, and the hedge of bean-vines near by was not strong enough to keep away wicked thoughts; his hot hands wilted the cool grass on which they lay, and his hot brain withered and blackened all that came into it.

He saw a good many boys dressed in fine clothes, and with shining curls down their shoulders, riding by in splendid coaches; and some of them held up their white hands tauntingly when they saw his tawny ones lying on the grass,—some even sneered at his garden, and said they had much better ones at home. Among the other passers, however, there came one day an old man that looked exceedingly sad, and who was terribly bowed down, and who, when he saw Ligie, called to his coachman to stop; and when his prancing horses stood still, champing their silver bits, spoke to him in words so friendly and so strange that he knew not what to make of it. And no wonder

Ligie knew not what to make of it, for, among other
things, the old man asked him whether he would
not like to be rich, and if he would sell his garden
for a piece of gold as big as his mother's house.
Ligie said nothing would make him so happy; to
which the old man replied that he did not want
the garden, but that he would give him all the
gold he wanted if he would consent to perform for
him a trifling service; and when Ligie asked what
it was, and learned that it was only the carrying
of a small burden, he readily agreed to go with
the old man. It would be easier than working in
the garden, he thought, — O, anything would be
easier than that! and then to have all the gold he
wanted, — surely, he could not suffer, no matter
what he had to do; so, with a bound, he sprang
from the grass and into the coach; the door closed,
the silver latch shut with a snap, and his mother's
house was hid from him forever. At first he cared
very little about this; fortune was his and the
great world before him; could he not buy a great
palace if he chose, and why should he fret about
a poor little cottage in a scarcely-heard-of village?
And as for the garden, why, he should be glad
never to see it; and, for all he knew, his riches
would procure him the pleasure of walking in the
king's garden, and his roses and hops he supposed
were poor affairs compared with the king's roses

and hops; probably he should see birds as big as eagles before nightfall, — birds that would make the little brown twitterers at home stay there for shame; and he was surprised as they rode on and on to meet no such birds, and to see no prettier flowers than he had left at home.

But one thing surprised him more than the fact of meeting no birds as big as eagles, — the old man by whose side he rode gave him no burden to carry. At last he ventured timidly to suggest it, for he feared he was not earning his pleasure. "By and by," said the old man, and that was all.

Directly, however, he began to be secretly glad that no burden was given him, and to say in his heart, "Perhaps the old man will forget it altogether, and I have the gold all for nothing"; for when one bad thought got into his mind, a thousand others ran in behind it.

"What a good thing I have done," he kept saying, as they went along; "everybody that sees me will envy me, and won't that make me proud and happy!"

That night he slept in a richly-furnished chamber, where perfumes that seemed to him sweeter than roses loaded the air, and where a brilliant light burned at the head of the bed he slept on, — a bed greatly softer than the one he had left at home.

In the morning a rich repast was served to him on shining plate; he had not only meat and honey, but wine, and stronger drink than wine.

The second day an immense distance was traversed; and once or twice, when the motion of the coach grew tiresome, Ligie thought he heard a voice in him saying, "You might as well have stayed at home, little boy!" And each time he drowned it by inquiring of the old man whether he should not now take the burden agreed upon. "By and by," the old man said, and that was all. "He is a very strange man," thought Ligie; and, turning to look at him, he perceived, for the first time, that there was no smile in his face and no light in his eyes, and that his skin was dried like parchment and wrinkled as though it was drawn over dry bones. His hair was very white, and it seemed to Ligie as though it had been dead a long time. Happening to touch one of his fingers, he found it so cold that, shivering, he shrank away. Then first the old man smiled, — a grim, sarcastic smile, as if the child's motion were one he was well used to, and expected.

Ligie feared he had offended, and the mysterious voice said to him very plainly now, "You had better have stayed at home." "No, no," replied Ligie, "I am glad I came away"; but they were only words, and the feeling of gladness was not in his

heart. Then came the thought of his mother, and
with it a pain shot through his bosom, — a pain
that was not only sharp, but hot as fire. "If you
please, sir, I will take the burden," he said; "I
am getting tired of doing nothing." The old man
smiled again, and answered, "By and by," and
that was all.

Day after day they travelled so together, — the
old man silent and sad, and the boy growing impatient, and tired of the everlasting motion and noise
of the close-shut coach in which they rode. Night
after night he slept in a soft bed, and morning after
morning was served with dainties more dainty than
he had ever imagined; but after a few weeks he
began to think of the plain fare at home with regret. Then the voice laughed, and said, "Fool
that you were to come away!" and this time poor
Ligie could make no answer.

And day after day he asked the old man to allow
him to carry the burden agreed upon, and day
after day the old man replied, "By and by," and
that was all.

At last the rolling and swinging of the coach
made him sick, the healthful color went from his
cheek, and all the strength he used to have seemed
to forsake him. The time was come that people
looked enviously upon him as he rode along; but
so far from gratifying, it but added to Ligie's dis-

comfort; no one thought of giving him love and sympathy now, he could very well afford to do without them, so they who saw him believed. Poor Ligie! the less he was pitied, the more he pitied himself; and so, day after day, and week after week, he and the old man journeyed on and on, searching for pleasure which they never found. So weary grew Ligie at length, that he resolved to quit the old man, who had never given him the proposed burden, but still said, "By and by," whenever reminded of it; and one day, seeing him asleep, and his gray hair fallen low about his eyes, the wretched child softly unlocked the coach-door, and made haste to be gone, or tried to make haste, for, to his horror, he found that it was with the greatest difficulty he could move at all. His limbs were as limbs asleep, and his back was doubled down almost like the old man's back.

"So ho!" exclaimed his mysterious companion, "you repent your bargain, do you? Well, I am sorry, but a bargain is a bargain; I never fail to fulfil mine."

"How can you say that?" said Ligie; "have I not been with you the longest year that was ever made, and where is the burden I was to carry? I can't live this way any longer, for doing nothing is the hardest work I ever did."

Then the old man laughed aloud, and said, "My

son, you have the burden already ; it is that that
weighs you down."

"It is not true," answered Ligie ; and he unfolded
his arms to convince the old man that he had no
burden ; but he only shook his head incredulously,
and added, "You have it concealed ; it is the way
rich people carry burdens."

Ligie was now angry, and opened his clothing
even to his bosom, to convince the old man that he
concealed nothing.

"You have it for all that," was the reply ; "and
because of it you cannot lift yourself up."

Then Ligie grew pale, and trembled, saying,
"How can I have a burden which I cannot see ?"

"Is pain the less certain because you cannot see
it ?" the old man said.   "I did not stipulate
whether you were to carry the burden in your
arms, or on your head, or in your heart"; and he
smiled a smile half bitterness and half sadness as
he spoke.

Then came the truth crushing through Ligie's
senses, — the burden was in his heart ; and cover-
ing his face with his hands, he cried a long while.

"In mercy," said the old man, "I gave you
little by little ; but it was none the less sure, and
'By and by' has come."

The low voice never spoke so clearly as it spoke
now, saying, "O mistaken youth, you have sold

your birthright for a mess of pottage!" "O terrible, terrible voice, why do you torment me?" said Ligie; and the voice answered, "Such is my work."

After a season of despair, however, Ligie began to imagine, very foolishly, that strong drink and strong pleasures would dissolve the stone which he was persuaded had been wickedly gotten into his heart. Without sorrow on the part of either, he and his friend — if friend he might be called — took separate ways. True to his foolish imaginings, he saw dances, and heard music, and drank wine, and stronger drink than wine, and bought great houses and much land, gazed on fine pictures, some of them painted by the greatest artists in the world; but, through all, Ligie remembered his mother's little house and garden with painful regret, and over all he heard the low voice reproaching him. He even came to walk in the king's garden, and to speak familiarly with princes; but they seemed to him not unlike other men, and even for their praises he felt none the better, but, while they smiled, often found his thoughts travelling away to the obscure village of Heatherford, and when he drank wine it seemed to him not so sweet as the cool water of his mother's well.

All his childish dream was fulfilled, — he had waked to find his pillow a pillow of gold; but he would gladly have given it for the pillow of common down which his mother's hands used to make so pleasant; nevertheless, something held him back. Was he ashamed to have his rich friends know that he was born in a low, little house, and that his mother was a poor woman? I am afraid so.

Years and years went by, and the little gardener was a little gardener no more; and thicker than the years crowded upon each other crowded the wrinkles in his face; and before the pleasure he sought was found, his hair grew white as the frost, and his step slow as the sloth.

Celebrated waters he plunged into, and hired with much gold physicians of great repute to treat his malady, which, in spite of all their skill, grew only the worse; indeed, it seemed to Ligie sometimes that the stone in his heart was grown to be a mountain.

And all the night and all the day the voice within him said to him, " Go home, Ligie "; and all the night and all the day Ligie said to the voice, " At the new year, or in the spring-time, or when the leaves fall, I will go." And still, as he sailed in vessels or rode on cushions, his prayer was for the feet of his lost youth and the strength of his lost youth, to walk as he used to do. Often he tried to walk, feeling his way along with a stick; but he fancied

he frightened the birds and spoiled their songs, for
sure was he they sang not as they used to sing
among the sweet-smelling hops of his mother's garden.   The little boys that were laughing and kick-
ing up the dust stopped their playing as he came
near, and gazed on him with eyes full of fear, instead of sunshine.   If flowers fringed the wayside,
their tops seemed dusty and dry, and not dewy and
sweet as they used to be.   The young girl who sat
singing her ditty at the window, when she saw his
frowning visage and bent form, drew in her breath
and her music, and hastily pulled down the sash.

The very cattle ran away from him, stopping not
till the width of the meadow in which they pas-
tured was between themselves and him.   The hens
left their peeping broods and crept away, afraid to
fly at him as they did at the urchin who plagued
them.

Seeing the sorry effect he had upon bird and
beast, he grew more and more dissatisfied, and the
burden in his heart weighed heavier and heavier
upon him.

Something like the shadow of gladness passed
over him, when in a valley before him he saw rising
the spires of a quiet village.   "I will abide here,"
he said, " and try if the air will not soften this terrible stone."   So he hired a house, and physicians,
and attendants, and made himself a home, but

found little of the peace he sought.   Consternation ran up and down the streets, when it was known among the people that an old man with a stone in his heart would thenceforth abide among them, for the physicians pronounced his malady not only incurable, but the most infectious of all diseases ; so the attendants he had went away from him, and all his gold could not hire others in their places.   In vain he sought religious comfort ; the clergyman to whom he applied was of the opinion that Ligie had not only a stone in his heart, but that he had a demon there, into the bargain ; and this was certainly poor consolation.

Then the doctors resolved that the poor man should not go abroad any more, for there was never such fright as the stone and the demon occasioned.

When the doomed man was informed of the verdict, he said it was just and right, and he furthermore admitted that when he listened he could hear a voice within him that condemned him.   Then the wise men recommended entire abstinence from all exertion of mind and body, and constant listening to the condemning voice, with as much meditation on the stone as possible.

And all the people exclaimed, " Yea, verily, these physicians are wiser men than till now we knew them to be ! " and their fame stood before them like a light that made common people almost afraid.

Poor Ligie submitted patiently to the treatment, and also to separation from all human society, and found all the satisfaction he had in hugging his woes. However, he grew no better. Sometimes he would creep to his windows, and indulge in the harmless occupation of looking into the sunshine; but this habit was no sooner discovered than it was resolved by the people that the man with the stone in his heart should be put in irons for the first offence, and that for the second he should be imprisoned for life.

" He has already offended twice," said one of the most fearful; and upon himself he took the administration of justice, and, stealing to the old man's house in the night, secured the door with a ponderous bar.

It was dreadful to hear the prisoner's moans after that; no one who heard them once could be induced to go near him again; so he lay moaning and groaning to himself. Some of the more superstitious believed it was the demon that cried, and not the man himself; but there were some who thought a stone in the heart was enough to make anybody moan.

" We shall have to break his heart, and so free it from the stone," said the surgeon; and but for an accident it is likely the cruel suggestion might have been carried out.

An old woman, residing in the suburbs of the town, remarkable for nothing but industry, modesty, and strong common sense, chanced to come near this old man's house one stormy midnight, as she was returning home from having dressed a corpse. She had gone abroad so little, and been so given to minding her own affairs, that she had never once heard of the old man with a stone in his heart, and came fearlessly to the very door. The moon shone bright and friendly through the chinks, and as she peeped in she saw the glitter of two eyes that looked like the eyes of a famished wolf.

In vain the prisoner cried out to her to flee away, saying he had a great stone in his heart, and was possessed of a demon ; the assertion sounded so much like nonsense to the ears of the old woman, she refused to go, and furthermore the glitter of the man's eyes told plainly enough that he was starving ; so, notwithstanding his entreaties that she should leave him to his fate, and save herself, she made haste to unbar the door, and, walking straight to the straw where he lay, bade him arise and go with her.

At first he refused, saying that he had a stone in his heart, and a demon in his bosom, and that to go with her was impossible.

" Ah, yes," said the old woman, " I see how it is," for she knew that too much brooding on light

THE MAN WITH A STONE IN HIS HEART.

afflictions will sometimes produce heavy ones, and
was resolved to humor his disease in order to cure
it. "I know a great witch who can cure you,"
she said ; " there is not a doubt of it ; she has
brought many back to health and happiness, whose
minds were gone far astray, and whose feet were
near the borders of the grave. Rise quickly, and
come along with me."

The old man lifted himself on one elbow, and
said he had tried all remedies in vain, and that he
had no courage for a new trial ; but though he
said he had no courage, he smiled faintly, and felt
a very little courage.

"Ah, it is not such medicine as you have been
used to with which the witch cures," said the old
woman ; " it is with a charm known only to herself, said to be the pleasantest thing in the world."

She spoke hopefully and cheerfully, and the man
answered, "Let us go to her at once," and he
arose, and looked with shining, hungry eyes close
in the old woman's face ; and, taking his limber,
weak, and worthless hands in hers, she led him out
of his miserable den, and they took their way together through the village, and struck into a sweet-
scented clover-field, lighted by the clearest and
brightest of moons.

As they went along, Ligie told of the many
things he had suffered in the hope of cure, and

that withal he had grown worse and worse, till he had come to be the miserable creature she beheld.

At first the old woman was obliged to walk very slowly ; but gradually she quickened her steps, and, unaware, her companion quickened his, too ; and as he walked faster and faster he straightened himself more, and when they reached the nice little home where the woman lived he stood nearly upright.

The first care of the nurse was to feed her patient with plain but wholesome and nutritious food ; and this done, she made him a bed, very clean and comfortable, where he slept soundly till morning.

His first inquiry on waking was for the witch, and his first desire was for an immediate interview.

" The witch lives a good way off," said the nurse, " and to leave home for so long a journey, I must needs make some preparation ; and if you will consent to help a little, only a very little, I shall be ready so much the sooner."

Ligie said he had not done a chore for years ; nevertheless, he would attempt whatever task she would set for the sake of being brought so much the sooner to the witch. So the old woman took him to the garden, and set him to weeding the beds there ; and as he worked he gained strength to work, so before noon the garden-beds were as clean as they could be.

When the old woman came out and saw what he had done, she was well pleased, and said she had never found so good a gardener in her life ; and she added, " We will soon be ready for the journey at this rate."

Ligie was a good deal tired and a little hungry with the work, and when the nurse brought a platter containing bread and fruit and meat, and placed it on a bench that stood in a shady place, he quite forgot in the enjoyment of it the stone in his heart ; and after the meal he forgot it for an hour longer in the pleasant sleep that came to him as he lay on the cool, grassy bed that Nature had made for him.

Toward sunset the old woman appeared, and directed her patient to cut off all the ends of the bean-vines that were trailing from the tops of the poles toward the ground.

When Ligie hesitated, and said he could not lift himself up for such work, she encouraged him to believe that he might straighten himself sufficiently for the task, and assured him of the impossibility of making the journey to the witch's house till the bean-vines were attended to. Hearing this, he lifted himself up, and began to clip off the ends of the bean-vines. They were sweet with blossoms, reminding him of the old garden at home ; and in the interest of his occupation, he thought nothing about the terrible crook in his back, and when at last he felt for it, it was gone.

He began now to think his hostess was the witch who had charmed the stone out of his heart, and from that time manifested no unwillingness to do whatever she bade.

Day by day she set him harder tasks, professing all the time when such a tree was felled, and such a field ploughed, or the orchard-trees pruned, or some other task accomplished, she would journey with him to the witch's house. But the work stretched itself out before Ligio as far as he could see; for while he gathered apples he saw the corn ripening, and of itself breaking out of the husk; and as he thought more about his work he thought less about the witch, and finally began to conclude there was no such thing in the world as a witch.

At last the heap in the crib was rounded up with the last golden ears, the oxen turned loose among the corn-stalks, and a bright wood-fire made on the hearth of the good old woman's house. In the middle of the floor the table was spread with pumpkin-pies, and apple-tarts, and sweetcakes, and all the variety which a country housewife knows so well how to provide. All the friends of the old woman had been invited to rejoice with her over the restoration of her patient; but, strange to say, where one came there were a dozen who stayed

away, for they now feared the harmless old woman
as much as they had formerly feared Ligie.   If he
was cured of stone in the heart, she must be a witch,
that was all ; so hard is it for us to believe in the
virtue of simple things, and that we have only to
wash and be clean.   If Ligie had done some great
thing, then it would have been easy to believe.

" O, if my mother were here to rejoice with me,
how happy I should be ! " sighed Ligie, as he concluded reflections not unlike what I have written ;
" for though I am old and worn and weary, I
might yet do much good ; but. how much more
might I have done if in youth I had improved my
opportunities, instead of wasting them in vain and
foolish dreaming and repining, — dreaming of impossible things, and repining that good things were
not the best things ! "

Then in his mind he made a picture of his
mother's little house he had once so come to de-
spise, and of the garden he had grown so tired of,
and it seemed to him that the king's garden was
not half so beautiful, that Eden itself could not
have been so beautiful.   In the light of memory
the loveliness, which in reality he had failed to see,
came out clear and distinct, and he marvelled that
he could have received such blessings and been so
unconscious of them.

Tears came to his eyes, and in the anguish of

9   M

repentance he wept aloud, saying over and over, "O, to have back my lost youth!" Then it was he seemed to hear, between his sobbings, a voice like his mother's, saying, "My son, my dear, little son!"

A thrill of joy ran through him, which was as if all the heavens had opened, and in the rapture of the moment he awoke, — for he had been all this time in a dream, — awoke to find himself little Ligie, and to see the sunset shadows on the water of the spring, that flowed from its fountain under the willow-tree, by which he remembered to have thrown himself at noonday. But when he was fully awake the thrill of joy kept still thrilling through his bosom; it was not all a dream; he heard the sweet voice of his mother still saying, "My dear, little son," and all the beauty he had seen shining so clearly in the light of memory he saw shining all round about him.

Over a bank of golden clouds the sun was peeping and smiling his good-night, the birds were hushing in the hop-vines and under the roses, and under his feet the grass was cool and green as it could be. In the distance stood dark, leafy woods, with cows and sheep and lambs feeding along the hills.

But the brightest spot of all the picture was the little house under the apple-tree, and with the

morning-glory at the window, and the red creep-
ers over the porch, where stood his mother smiling, and calling, "Ligie, my son, my dear, little
son!"

You may be sure he lingered not long even for
the sake of the beautiful landscape, glorified as it
was by the last red light of the day, and the first
white light of the stars, but ran at once up the
smooth path between the lilacs and lady-slippers,
answering, "I am coming, mother, I am coming!" it was as if he had new feet and new hands
and new senses; as if a new world had been made
about him; as if, indeed, a great stone had been
taken out of his heart. There was the table spread
in the middle of the floor with cakes and apple-
tarts and meat and milk, just as he had dreamed,
and his hair was all unfaded, and his limbs strong
and full of health.

What more could he have? Nothing, nothing.
Ligie felt this, and clasping his hands, he bowed
his head, and said, "How good God is, and how
unmindful and bad we are!"

And seeing how his spirit was changed, his
mother inquired of him what had happened; and
when he told her all his dream, and his thoughts
previous to the dream, they laughed and wept together, and wished that everybody could have such
a dream, and learn by it to appreciate the blessings

they have, rather than mourn for those they have not; and to work with willing hands and a resolute will in whatever field their portion may be cast.

CATY JANE.

ONE summer morning, as I walked
  Along a shady lane,
I met a black-eyed little girl,
  Whose name was Caty Jane.

She had a pretty basket full
  Of blossoms blue and white,
And when I asked her where she went,
  She hid her face from sight;

And sitting where the clover grew
  So sweet and thick and red,
She said, " I had a sister once
  Who loved me, and is dead;

" And yonder, to the slope on which
  You see the willows wave,
I 'm going with my flowers, for there
  Is little Annie's grave.

"Her goodness and her gentleness
  I oftentimes forgot;
She never said an unkind word, —
  I wish that I had not.

"We had a play-house once, beside
  This very shady lane;
I wish it never had been made,"
  Said little Caty Jane.

"'T was carpeted with grass, and weeds
  Were piled to make the walls;
The beds were spread with burdock-leaves,
  And mother gave us dolls.

"We had some broken cups, and had
  Some skeins of thread, I know,
And sometimes we pretended we
  Were women, and would sew;

"And often I would visit her,
  And she would come again,
And make believe to visit me,"
  Said little Caty Jane.

"One day, when cloudily the sun
  Was going down the hill,
Dear Annie said, 'We must go home,'
  The wind was growing chill.

" And when she wrapt her apron round
    Her neck and shoulders bare,
I laughed, and called her grandmamma,
    And said it was n't fair

" 'That she should run away, nor care
    For playing, nor for me.
' O Caty Jane,' said Annie, then,
    ' I 'm cold as I can be.

" 'It seems as if no fire nor quilt
    Could make me warm again.'
And, sure enough, they never did,"
    Said little Caty Jane.

" She said that more and more her head
    Kept aching all the while,
And from her hands the playthings fell,
    But still she tried to smile.

" And when the moon came up and shone
    So cold across the floor,
She said that we would never play
    Together any more.

" ' Well, if you feel so very bad,
    Do let 's go home,' said I,
' That you may have a chance to make
    Your will before you die.'

" And so I ran and left her in
   Our play-house by the lane,
And ran the faster when she called,
   ' Don't leave me, Caty Jane.'

" And sitting by the warm wood-fire,
   In little Annie's chair,
I fell asleep, and woke in fright, —
   My sister was n't there.

" ' She must be in a neighbor's house,'
   My mother said ; but I
Hid in her lap my face, and cried
   As hard as I could cry ;

" And told her I had left her in
   Our play-house by the lane ;
And there they found her, sure enough,"
   Said little Caty Jane,

" Lying upon the frozen ground,
   As cold as cold could be;
And when I called her pretty names
   She did not speak to me.

" But with pale cheek and shut eyes lay
   Upon our little bed.
And when the sun arose at morn,"
   Poor mourning Caty said,

"I called her to get up, and kissed
　　Her cheek to make her wake ;
And when she did not speak nor smile,
　　I thought my heart would break.

"I brought my playthings and my dolls,
　　And laid them on the bed,
And told her they were hers to keep,"
　　Poor little Caty said.

"And, waiting there in fear and doubt,
　　They softly kissed my brow,
And told me I must live without
　　My sister Annie, now.

"O then I knew how dear she was,"
　　Said little Caty Jane,
"And thought if she could be alive,
　　And play with me again,

"I 'd say a thousand things to her
　　That I had never said.
'T was easy work to think kind words
　　To say when she was dead."

And with her eyes brimful of tears,
　　She went along the lane ;
No sister now had she to love, —
　　Poor little Caty Jane !

Seeing how very long she stayed
  By Annie's lonesome bed,
I thought, If other little girls,
  Whose sisters are not dead,

Could know how blest they are, and see
  The sad look Caty wore,
They never would be heard to speak
  A cross word any more.

For we must do to others just
  As we would be done by,
If we would learn to live in peace,
  Or peacefully to die.

THE STREET BEGGAR.

SHAKE not your glossy curls with a " No,"
  As you sit in the warm and rosy glow
'Twixt your hearth and pictured wall ;
Ah, my lady, you do not know
How folk feel with their feet in the snow,
  And no bright fire at all.

A sixpence ! that you will never miss ;
See what a baby you have to kiss,
  Honor and wealth to prove ;
Ah, my lady, you cannot guess
  9 *

How folk feel in a night like this,
    With no little child to love.

From house to house I have gone all day, —
"Nothing for beggars," is all they say,
    Though a banquet waiting stands;
Ah, you never have known the way
Poor folk feel when their heads are gray
    And palsy shaking their hands.

For sake of charity say not "No."
I am almost famished, — I cannot go, —
    I must steal or starve, — and why?
Because, my lady, you do not know
How folk feel with their feet in the snow,
    Turned out from your fires to die.

EVIL CHANCE.

WHEN falls the hour of evil chance, —
    And hours of evil chance will fall, —
Strike, though with but a broken lance, —
    Strike, though you have no lance at all.

Shrink not, whate'er the odds may be, —
    Shrink not, however dark the hour, —
The barest possibility
    Of good deserves your utmost power.

PLEA FOR THE BOYS.

YOUNG men must work, and old men rest,—
  They have earned their quiet joys;
And everywhere, from east to west,
  The boys must still be boys.

They do not want your larger sight,
  Nor want your wisdom grim:
The boy has right to the boy's delight,
  And play is the work for him.

The idle day is the evil day,
  And work in its time is right;
But he that wrestles best in the play
  Will wrestle best in the fight.

Then do not, as their hour runs by,
  Their harmless pleasures clip;
For he that sails his kite to the sky
  May sometime sail a ship.

And soon enough the years will steal
  Their mood of frolic joys;
So keep your shoulder to the wheel,
  And let the boys be boys.

WORK.

DOWN and up and up and down, —
  Over and over and over, —
Turn in the little seed, dry and brown,
  Turn out the bright red clover!
Work, and the sun your work will share,
  And the rain in its time will fall,
For Nature, she worketh everywhere,
  And the grace of God through all.

With hand on the spade and heart in the sky,
  Dress the ground and till it ;
Turn in the little seed, brown and dry,
  Turn out the golden millet ;
Work, and your house shall be duly fed,
  Work, and rest shall be won ;
I hold that a man had better be dead
  Than alive, when his work is done !

Down and up and up and down,
  On the hill-top, low in the valley ;
Turn in the little seed, dry and brown,
  Turn out the rose and the lily.
Work with a plan, or without a plan,
  And your ends they shall be shaped true ;
Work, and learn at first-hand, like a man,
  The best way to *know* is to *do!*

Down and up till life shall close,
   Ceasing not your praises ;
Turn in the wild, white, winter snows,
   Turn out the sweet, spring daisies.
Work, and the sun your work will share,
   And the rain in its time will fall,
For Nature, she worketh everywhere,
   And the grace of God through all.

COUNSEL.

THOUGH sin hath marked thy brother's brow,
   Love him in sin's despite,
But for his darkness, haply thou
   Hadst never known the light.

Be thou an angel to his life,
   And not a demon grim ;
Since with himself he is at strife,
   O be at peace with him.

Speak gently of his evil ways,
   And all his pleas allow ;
For since he knows not why he strays
   From virtue, how shouldst thou ?

Love him, though all thy love he slights,
   For ah, thou canst not say

But that his prayerless days and nights
    Have taught thee how to pray.

Outside themselves all things have laws,
    The atom and the sun;
Thou art thyself, perhaps, the cause
    Of sins which he has done.

If guiltless thou, why surely then
    Thy place is by his side, —
It was for sinners, not just men,
    That Christ the Saviour died.

THE END.

Cambridge : Stereotyped and Printed by Welch, Bigelow, & Co.